Also by J. A. Castagno

Octavia and the Greek Key

Lady of the Lantern

The Fugitive Series - Coming in early 2016

Witness to Terror

Out of Tunis

DANCE OF THE RED PANEL

J. Anthony Castagno
A Novella

This is a work of fiction. All characters, businesses, places, events or incidents either are the products of the author's imagination or used in a fictitious manner. Any resemblance to actual persons, living or dead, or actual events is purely coincidental.

Old soldiers never die; they just fade away.

General Douglas MacArthur

To my father, Amadeo Castagno, a paratrooper who served his country and became the First Sergeant of Bravo Company, 1ˢᵗ Battalion, 504ᵗʰ Parachute Infantry Regiment during World War II. After three combat parachute jumps in Sicily, Italy and Holland, he would go on to fight in Korea and in Vietnam with his son in 1968.

Chapter I

THE SICILY DROP

The night of July 10, 1943, Second Lieutenant Jackson peered into the moonless sky outside the open door of the twin engine C-47 Skytrain, a thousand feet above the Mediterranean Sea.

The glow of the bright red jump light near the edge of the doorframe cast a surreal hue across his face. He looked at two planes, in formation, next to his. The closest flew less than a hundred feet away, the second trailed at a slightly higher altitude. Over a hundred and forty planes, carrying 1,600 paratroopers of the 504th Parachute Infantry Regiment, headed toward the coast of Sicily. His men were about to leap into combat, and a thousand questions bounced around inside Jackson's head.

May 10, 1943, when the regiment arrived in Casablanca on the USS George Washington, remained fresh in his memory. Tonight, two months later, he and his men headed for their first parachute jump of the war.

He ran his hand across the snaps on each of the four pockets and the dual-zippered switchblade knife pocket on the upper chest of his uniform. His index finger forced its way under his helmet's leather chinstrap cradling his jaw and clamping his teeth together. As he edged toward the door, his baggie jump pants flapped against his legs. Jackson's fingers clamped on the doorframe and he leaned into the prop blast. The whitecaps on the surface of the water looked as if they were less than two hundred feet below the belly of his plane. *Night, the water looks closer.*

Aware his men depended on him; he shoved himself away from the door and turned to the seventeen combat ready troopers seated along the sides of the plane. A mix of dull camouflage colors and designs painted the faces of the men, ranging in age from seventeen to forty. The smell of musty uniforms, profuse perspiration and recent vomit crept into his nostrils. His eyes turned to the sleeves of those on his right and focused on the bright red double 'A' shoulder patch of the 82nd Airborne Division. Each set of eyes in the plane fixed on him. *They're all scared shitless, wondering who will survive?* No one knew how long it would take to defeat the Axis armies and end the war. Jackson stared at the men and bit his lip. *Many of them may be dead soon.*

That same night, eighteen-year-old Seaman Dexter Kiddman, 'The Kid', could not shake the nickname given to him that day by his shipmates. Covered in sweat and grime, the baby-faced anti-aircraft gunner slumped in the hard metal seat of his four-barreled gun. His bewildered gaze focused on the blue phosphorescent wave tops and faint silhouettes of blacked out American and British warships, in formation off the coast of Sicily. Ten minutes earlier, German planes had attacked and bombed the fleet. *We're lucky we didn't get hit.*

Dexter shook sweat from his face, rubbed his burning eyes and picked out small dots emerging along the dark horizon. *Damn, I spoke too soon.* His heart pounded in his chest and emptiness crept into his stomach. Adjusting himself in his seat, he directed his attention to the circular spots low in the sky. The small images grew larger and transformed into a formation of planes on a direct path toward his ship. He wiped his trembling hands on his pants and reached for the circular hand crank. The muscles of his hands tensed as he turned the wheel to elevate the barrels of the gun, shook cobwebs from his brain and looked at the man next to him peering through the sight. *More German bombers, coming in low. When will they stop?* It seemed like a half hour passed although it took two minutes for the planes to come into range. Dexter's fingers tightened on the crank as the barrels erupted. Men behind him fed ammunition to the weapon and a chain reaction began. Sailors on nearby ships took their cue and opened fire on the approaching planes.

Lieutenant Jackson stood near the jump door and watched tracer bullets chase each other past the plane. Explosions left black puffs of smoke in and around the Skytrain formation. Below the plane, he saw the black silhouettes of ships firing into the sky. He bit the inside of his cheek and concealed the fear racing through his body.

After flashing the okay sign to his men, he shuffled back to the door and saw a nearby plane catch fire. Wide eyed, he froze staring at the burning C-47 as its nose dropped and the flaming inferno spun toward the open sea. A sudden bright light brought him out of his trance. Shrapnel ripped into his chest. Both his hands pressed against the wound and he stumbled toward his men. Their expressions of shock made him glance at his hands and the blood seeping between his fingers.

The trembling soldiers, weighted down with equipment, helped each other scramble from their seats. They struggled to hook parachute static lines to a cable and ran toward the door. An explosion ripped open the side of the plane.

During the night of July 11 and throughout, the next day, word of the disaster, spread among the men of the regiment. Mid-morning on July 13, the bright sun, in a cloudless sky, beat down on three members in Bravo Company, of the 1st Battalion. They trudged toward the light Mediterranean surf on a small Sicilian beach below a cliff. Each wore the distinctive airborne, cotton twill, jump jacket and canvas reinforced baggy pants.

Twenty-four-year old Staff Sergeant Antonio 'Tony' DeMarco adjusted the M2 Carbine slung over his shoulder and glanced back at the two men following him in the rocky cove. One of his squad leaders, Sergeant Alfonzo 'Al' Bertone, with a Thompson sub-machine gun across his chest like a bass guitar sung on a short strap, celebrated his twenty first birthday a week ago. Behind Al, marched Private First

Class John Rivers, a seventeen-year-old southern Alabama native, carrying his M1 Garand rifle cradled in one arm. Tony smiled. *He thinks it's his personal hunting rifle.*

"Who the hell picked us for this detail?" Al asked.

"Someone's gotta do it," Rivers said.

Tony shook his head. "Quit complaining, Al. If you were back at the tent, you would have lost next month's pay in the poker game with those guys from Alpha Company."

Small waves lapped across the trio's most treasured possession, their brown Corcoran jump boots, as they approached two bodies bobbing in the shallow surf. They stopped beside the dead paratroopers and did not make a sound. Tony pressed his lips together and shook his head.

Al made the sign of the cross.

A miserable end, just before the fight began. Tony thought. "Pull them up on the beach and get the dog tags. Rivers, write down this location."

Al and Rivers dragged the bodies to dry sand.

Al fished around a dead trooper's neck and located a chain. He removed one of the dog tags and looked at the name. "Poor bastard. We were lucky our plane didn't get hit." He held the remaining tag between two fingers and shoved it under the dead man's shirt.

Tony stuffed his hand into a pocket of his jump jacket and pulled out a dozen dog tags strung on parachute cord. He avoided looking at the names on the small pieces of metal and deep lines etched across his face before he turned to Rivers. The young soldier held a dog tag in front of his face and open mouth.

"Rivers, you don't have to memorize his name," Tony said.

Rivers' fair-skinned face turned ashen. "His name is John, same as mine."

Tony stared at him and shook his head. "Lotta guys named John will die in this war. You will not be one of them."

The two men handed Tony the dog tags. He strung each on the cord, tied a knot and crammed them into his jacket pocket. The folded red canvas protruding from his large pants pocket caught his eye. He shoved the canvas deeper into the cavity.

Chapter II

PLANS

Major Jim Franklin, the lanky Intelligence Officer of the 1st Battalion, 504th Parachute Infantry Regiment, shuffled his feet at the end of a large table. He looked around waiting for orders to start the briefing. Across the room, Captain Paul Wilson, Bravo Company Commander, and two other captains stood in a stiff, at ease position, near six lieutenants and majors. Franklin picked up a thin, three-foot long olive tree branch and scraped the few remaining pieces of bark from it with his fingernail.

A map of the southern Italian coast hung on the bullet-hole-ridden wall next to the table.

Franklin knew many men in the room referred to him as Doubting Jim, the regiment's pessimist. He never believed it would take just two months to rout the Germans from Sicily and chase them across the Strait of Messina. He swore he'd never again question the fighting ability of the often outnumbered and out-gunned paratroopers. *September 12ᵗʰ and we're planning to jump into Salerno tomorrow night.*

Franklin focused on the Regimental Commander, Colonel Turner, at the head of the table in a room dead with silence. The word timid did not exist in Turner's dictionary, but tenacity appeared multiple times in bold letters. *The soldiers in the regiment love the man.* He pushed people well beyond their comfort zone, barking orders in the true fashion of a leader, from the front. Turner did not attend battalion operations briefings often, but after the grim tragedy during the flight into Sicily, he took a personal interest in planning, down to the battalion level. With both elbows planted on the table, his steepled fingers pressed against each other while he stared at the tabletop and clamped his teeth on his bottom lip. To his right, Lieutenant Colonel Emery, the Battalion Commander, waited for his boss to speak.

Colonel Turner lifted his head. "Okay Jim, what's it look like?"

Franklin raised the branch, took a moment to decide which end to hold, and stepped to the map. He swung the homemade pointer and planted the tip on the coastline, south of Salerno. "The 36th Infantry Division is holding on by the skin of their teeth near Paestum, thirty miles south of Salerno. Division Operations staff doesn't know how much longer they can hold the beach."

Turner tapped his foot and rubbed his temple. "What are they up against?"

"The Germans are unorganized because of their retreat from Sicily. From what we can tell, they've gathered elements of the 29th Panzer Grenadier Division, the 26th Panzers and 2nd Parachute Division. They also have a small contingent of Tiger tanks from the Hermann Goering Division."

"What about any remaining Italian troops?" Turner asked.

"Most of them disappeared into the countryside when Italy surrendered four days ago."

Turner nodded. "Good. Now, what about their supplies and reinforcements? Where are the German troops coming from and what equipment are they receiving?"

Franklin raised his shoulders and eyebrows. "Everything they need is coming in from the north, sir. And more Tiger tanks from the Goering Division are on their way."

Turner placed both his hands flat on the table, glanced at the map and set his fingers in motion as if playing a piano. "Those are good size mountains to the east and northeast. They're not climbing over them. What passes might they be using?"

Franklin slid his makeshift pointer northeast of the beachhead. "Most likely this major road through the Picentini mountains, but we don't know for sure."

Turner cocked his head to the side and pursed his lips. "What about air reconnaissance? Anyone take a look at that area?"

"There's little or no air support available, sir." Franklin's insides churned when he swore he heard those across the room gasp. He waited for what he thought would be a gruff response. Everyone knew the colonel did not like to hear the words 'we can't' or 'there's not enough'.

Turner stared at Franklin and tightened his lips and jaw. He shoved an extended thumb over his shoulder. "What the hell are those planes parked outside along the runways?"

Emptiness grew in the pit of Franklin's stomach. He recalled the colonel had always been cordial to him, but he remembered stories of officers who uttered the wrong word and bore the brunt of a mad-dog ass chewing.

"The air corps guys are telling me they don't have enough tactical aircraft to get in low and fast. They won't use C-47's, they're too slow," Franklin said. He felt alone in the room and glanced at the officers standing to the side. None dared move a muscle. When he turned his head back to Turner and saw the smile on his face, he relaxed.

"Okay Jim. I have a job for you. It shouldn't take long. When we're done here, get me names and ranks of the flyboys. It's time their pressed uniforms get a little ruffled. I'll be lighting brush fires under a few asses this afternoon. Maybe that will get them in gear." Turner spent a moment chewing on the inside of his cheek and studying the wall map. "You think we could cut the German supply lines?"

"Yes, sir, if we can find them."

The colonel leaned back in his chair and made eye contact with each man in the room. "Where's the guy from the Italian resistance?"

"Outside," Franklin replied.

"Let's get him help and find out what they can do. I want a set of our eyes with him. Find a young stud who will blend in... and Franklin, check with the lost souls who seemed to have misplaced their airplanes. See if they have one of those air traffic control teams, we could use them up in the mountains."

"Will do, sir."

Turner and Emery stood and every man in the room came to attention. Turner supported his solid frame with both hands planted on the table. "We command America's best fighting men." He studied each officer and addressed the group. "On our Sicily jump, the US Navy and the British Navy shot down twenty three of our Skytrains loaded with my paratroopers. We lost almost two hundred and thirty men." He slammed a fist on the table. "It will not happen again, gentlemen." Turner marched toward the door and lowered his voice. "Never again will a mother bury her trooper son with an American bullet in him." Emery followed Colonel Turner out and shut the door.

Franklin dropped into a chair and exhaled, releasing the tension built up in his body over the last hour.

Everyone, except Captain Wilson and Franklin, gave Turner a thirty-second lead and walked out.

"Got a minute, sir?"

"Yeah, Wilson."

"I think I may have the answer to your problem."

"Which one? I'm loaded with them."

"I've got someone who would be good for the Italian resistance mission."

Franklin straightened in his chair. "Who?"

"Staff Sergeant Tony DeMarco. His lieutenant died going into Gela. He's leading one of my platoons until we get a replacement."

"Tony his first name?" Franklin asked.

"It's Antonio, sir."

"Is he Italian?"

"Yes, sir. I use him as a translator."

"Tell him what the old man wants and send him to see me."

"Right away, sir." Wilson headed to the door.

"Wilson!"

"Sir?"

"There's an Italian guy outside... in civilian clothes. Send him in here."

Franklin leaned back in his chair. None of the troops liked sitting around with nothing to do. After the fiasco at Gela, the US Army didn't know what to do with airborne units. *All we need is a good chance to prove this will work.*

The door opened and fifty-year-old Luca Amati headed to the table. Franklin didn't blame him for wearing brown pants and a tan shirt. No one wanted to be mistaken as a Fascist after Italy surrendered on September 8. A black shirt would raise suspicion with the Germans and the locals. *What better way to keep everyone off your ass.* He met Luca the day before, when the partisan arrived on a fishing boat out of the small village of Santa Maria di Castellabate, twenty miles south of the beachhead at Paestum. He smelled of fish from the covert boat ride. They spent three hours talking and Franklin grew to like the stocky partisan leader. He pointed to a chair.

"When your colonel walked out, he did not look happy," Luca said.

"He hates the United States and British Navy, but he'll get over it." Franklin did not expect Luca would press the issue. "I think we can help each other. I'll arrange for weapons and ammunition to be dropped to your men, but I want something in return."

Luca took a moment to study his shoes. "What is it?"

"Are your partisans free to move around in the mountains to the east?"

Luca grinned. "Free movement and the German army do not go together."

"Sorry, dumb question." He paused. *Get to the point.* "I need to get one of my men into the mountains. We want to find the route the Germans are using to bring in supplies. Can you help me?"

Luca clasped his hands behind his back and shook his head. "If the Germans see him, they will know he is an American. He would not have a chance."

"Maybe not," Franklin said.

###

Tony sat on the hard ground near the entrance to a twenty-man tent with a white 'B' painted above the doorway. *We got the dog tags, glad someone else is going back for the bodies.* He lifted an envelope and removed a photo of a man in a fedora. *He's getting old, hope he's okay.*

Sergeant Bertone, with a broad smile on his face, strolled around the corner of the tent. He dropped to one knee, slid a pack off his back, and removed a loaf of bread. "My aunt made this," he said ripping the load in half and handing a piece to Tony.

"So, you had a good time?"

"I did, all mornin wit family."

"Are they in that town outside Palermo?"

"Yeah, Alita, small place... not much there."

"Did they understand you?"

"One cousin spoke a little English and wit my broken Italian we did okay. Ya gotta teach me more words." He eyed the letter in Tony's hand. "We got mail? Anything fa me?"

"Not this time."

"Damn. My girl hasn't written for over a month."

"You need to go back to Alita. Your aunt can fix you up with a nice Sicilian cutie."

"The girl that helped her bake the bread was the prettiest thing I've seen in years."

Tony raised his eyebrows. "Did you get her name?"

"Sure, Antonella... she's my cousin."

Tony nodded and smiled. "If you go again, I'll go with you and you can introduce me to her."

"I've never seen you get mail from a girl."

"Haven't found one who can cook and shoot straight, but I'd love to take a look at your cousin Antonella."

Al pointed at the letter. "Ya get any good news?"

Tony grinned. *Folks back in the US don't understand what it's like over here.* "My father wants to know why I haven't seen my uncles and aunts." He shook his head. "On a hot day someone left the side door open at the Strand

Theater. From outside, he watched the news reel about Sicily... said I should take a jeep and drive to Salerno."

"Wish we were that close, but I don't think we're gettin in that fight," Al said.

A puffy cheeked private, in a uniform that looked like a blind tailor made it with an abundance of olive green cloth, ran around the corner of the tent. Tony did not recognize him but surmised he was a recruit in the middle of his first wartime mission.

"You guys in Bravo Company?" the private asked.

"Yeah," Al said, rolling his eyes at the painted 'B' on the tent, and leaving his customary 'dumb ass' off the end of his reply.

"Ya know Sergeant DeMarco?"

"That's me."

"Captain Wilson wants you to come to his tent."

Tony climbed to his feet, looked at the red canvas protruding from the side of his pants leg and shoved it deeper into the large pocket.

Al looked at him with a poker player's concerned face. "Damn Tony, you've been carryin that since we jumped, what the hell is it?"

Tony unfolded the canvas. "It's half of a drop zone marker panel." He whirled it above his head. "If I get cut off behind the lines, it'll attract attention."

Al grabbed the panel, imitated Fred Astaire's tap dance in the movie 'Broadway Melody', and waved it in the air. "Don't shoot the nut waving the red rag."

Tony caught the loose end, and they both held it in the air laughing. "It's the crazy Americans," Tony shouted. He pulled the panel from Al, folded it and shoved it back into the pocket.

Tony pushed back the flap hanging across the opening of the Officer's Wall Tent and looked at Captain Wilson sitting in one of two chairs at a small field desk. Seated, Wilson's eyes were less than a foot below Tony's eyes. Often, in a respectful way, he teased the captain, telling him the army needed to develop an oversized parachute with his name written on the risers.

"You wanna see me, sir?"

"Yeah Tony, have a seat. Where's your family in Italy?"

"In the mountains... a little east of Salerno."

"I guess you heard the Germans are kicking the shit out of our guys over there."

Waiting around in Sicily, while the battle raged in Italy, did not sit well with Tony. He and Captain Wilson served together since they went through jump school in late 1941. Over time, they both learned to speak their piece in private.

"Doesn't make much sense, captain. Why the hell are we sitting around in Sicily picking our noses and scratching our asses?"

"You haven't heard yet, we're going in tomorrow night. I was thinking about telling Lieutenant Kelly to keep an eye on your platoon."

"No problem, I can handle it, sir."

"Sure you can, but you may not be going with us."

What the hell did I do? Tony thought. His jaw tightened and his hands closed to fists. "You and I have been here from the beginning. Who's gonna stop me?"

"The colonel. He wants someone to jump in and help the Italian resistance."

Tony straightened in his chair and leaned over the table. "Where?"

"Southeast of Salerno."

The word Salerno filled his head, and his heart jumped in his chest. "I'll take it."

"Okay, get with Major Franklin at the conference room he set up for the battalion commander."

###

Tony opened the door to the makeshift conference room and marched to Major Franklin, mumbling to himself at the large table. He came to attention. "Staff Sergeant Tony DeMarco, sir."

Franklin pushed himself from the chair and extended his hand. "Nice to meet you, Sergeant. Did Captain Wilson tell you what we want?"

"Briefly."

"How good is your Italian?"

"Fluent, a dialect from around Salerno."

"Good. We need a volunteer to jump in and help the resistance. Are you interested? Think about it a second, it's not an easy mission."

Tony smiled. "Need not waste time thinking about it, sir. I'll go."

Franklin picked up the olive branch pointer and slung it across the room. He reached to the map and tapped it with his finger. "We've got a lot to talk about so let's get started. You'll jump in tomorrow night."

Tony's head spun and a hundred questions bounced around his inside his brain. Major Franklin did not keep him in the dark for long, they spent over an hour talking, asking each other questions and discussing the pro's and con's of the mission.

Tony turned the corner of the large tent. Al, asleep on the ground, did not look comfortable with the helmet pillow. He stopped beside him. "Al."

Al scrambled to his feet. "What happened? You've been gone more than an hour."

No one knew of the upcoming mission and Tony did not plan to be the one to broadcast the news. He turned his head looking from side to side and whispered. "I'm leaving tomorrow night."

"What about us?"

"Keep it quiet. The 1st Battalion jumps in around the same time."

"Ya meetin us on the drop zone?"

"No, I'm gonna help the partisans." He grinned and tapped the red canvas in his pants pocket. "Who knows? Might get to use this."

"Make sure ya wave it at the good guys."

Tony put his arm over Al's shoulder. "I will. Listen, take care of Rivers, he's still a kid. I don't want him getting hurt."

"He won't."

"I have to talk to Captain Wilson later. I'll put in a good word for you."

Chapter III

FRANCO

Tony's legs hung out the door of the light single engine plane six hundred feet above the Italian countryside. The wind pressed his body toward the interior of the plane. Hooked to a ring on the floor, his parachute static line flapped against the doorframe. He reached for its closed buckle and yanked. *It's secure,* he thought. All of his training had been with a platoon of motivated men. Now he faced going into battle with a small group of civilians who may not have any military training. They had one advantage over his men; they knew the countryside. *Guess I won't be speaking much English.*

The upcoming jump didn't concern him, the reception committee did. He gazed into the sky above the plane. "Please don't let the guys on the drop zone be Germans."

He felt a tap on his shoulder and turned to the pilot, pointing out the windshield. As he leaned out the door, he glanced at the moonless sky and studied the ground forward of the plane.

In a clearing, surrounded by trees, he spotted six small fires forming a cross on the ground. Tony scooted to the edge of the door and placed his hands on the floor beside his thighs. The jump, from such a low altitude, would offer him with little time to check his open parachute and prepare for a jarring impact with the ground. When the plane passed over the center of the cross, he shoved himself out the door.

Seconds after he hit the hard soil and rolled to his feet, he spotted a short man running toward him with a German MP-40 submachine gun draped across his chest. The man grabbed the parachute and pulled it to the ground. *If he was a German, I'd already be dead,* flashed through his mind as he unhooked his parachute harness.

The man released the parachute and ran to him. "I'm Luca Amati."

Two men stepped behind him and he turned to them. "Get his helmet. Take the parachute and the oil cans. I'll meet you tomorrow." He grabbed Tony's arm. "Come... quickly."

Tony adjusted his pack, clutched his M2 carbine with both hands, and raced into the trees with Luca. The butterflies in his stomach subsided.

Luca paid attention to his surroundings. He didn't look as if he wanted to hang around the drop zone to find out if the Germans saw the plane, and Tony didn't blame him.

During his briefing, Major Franklin explained everything to Tony's satisfaction. None of his questions went unanswered except how long it would take to complete the mission. *My life is in this guy's hands. Hope he's as good as Franklin said.* Tony stayed one-step to the side and a half step behind Luca.

Luca skirted open areas, making sure they remained hidden in the olive groves. In front of them, the terrain inclined into the mountains. For the next two hours, little talk between the two men interrupted the silence of the dark orchards.

Luca stopped and leaned against a tree. He removed a small cloth from his pocket and wiped sweat from his forehead. "Your name is Antonio?"

"Yeah, everyone calls me Tony."

"And you have family in Italy?"

"In Ponte, outside Salerno."

"I buy olives there. Rest a few minutes."

Tony removed the canteen from his belt and handed it to Luca. He studied the man in front of him. *Franklin said he was fifty Doesn't look that old, he's in good shape.* "Where are we going?"

"To my brother's house... an hour from here. He's dead... Franco's there." Luca passed the canteen to Tony.

"Who will help me?"

"Franco and Dario."

Tony scanned the trees and rocked from side to side alternating his weight on his legs. "How well do they know these mountains?"

"No one knows them better. The house is not far, we need to go."

Luca led them to the foot of a hill and pointed. "Just over this rise."

For the next forty-five minutes, they trudged up the incline. *Over a mile is not far to him.* Tony wiped beads of sweat from his face.

When they reached the crest, Tony looked down on a stone farmhouse in a clearing. A light flickered in the large window overlooking the front yard.

He studied the square house and the surrounding area. Two rock and concrete outbuildings sat behind it. At the corner of the house stood a thirty-foot tall tree, surrounded by white flowers. *Nice place for someone to hide.* At the front of the house, a dirt road passed the property, and from it, a cart path led to the front yard. "What's in those buildings out back?"

"Farm equipment and olive oil."

"You make it?"

Luca nodded and smiled. "The Amati family business for over a hundred years."

Luca led them down the steep slope and approached the tree line.

Tony's stomach quivered and pulse increased when they stepped from the trees, into an open area, in front of the house.

The sound of a rifle bolt sliding into place stopped Tony's heart, and adrenalin shot through his bloodstream. Near a pile of wood stacked against a wall, movement caught his eye. The urgency to assess and eliminate the threat overrode his need to take cover. His jaw tightened and sensitivity to his surroundings increased. "Down!" He motioned to Luca, dropped to one knee and raised his carbine toward the woodpile.

"No!" Luca lunged at him and shoved the muzzle of the weapon toward the ground. "It's Dario."

A young man holding a German bolt-action rifle emerged from the shadows along the side of the house. Tony furrowed his brow and squinted at the man, his mind racing in search of answers. Tall blond Dario would pass for a poster boy member of Hitler's Aryan race.

Tony shoved himself from the ground. "Jesus, I could have killed him. You should have told me he'd be waiting."

Luca lifted his shoulders and pursed his lips. He tapped Tony's shoulder. "Dario, this is the American soldier, Tony."

Dario said nothing, no 'hello', no 'how are you', no 'nice to meet you', not even 'I don't give a shit' passed from his lips. He cradled his rifle across his arm and raised his head jutting his chin forward. "You were the one who almost died." He trudged toward the house.

Tony sighed and wished he could burn a hole into Dario's back with his two eyes. "Great welcome. Not friendly is he?"

"I'll talk to him," Luca said.

Tony lost sight of Dario when he turned the corner of the house. *He doesn't act or look Italian.* He slung his rifle over his shoulder and confronted Luca. "Six foot tall and blond hair?"

"His mother is from the North."

Luca led Tony through the front door and into a living room.

An oil lantern cast dim light across the room and reflected off the polished walls. *Nice place.* Tony scanned the room. To his side, a couch sat in front of the window overlooking the yard. A large table and chairs stood against a wall. On the table, he counted four wine bottles standing in a line. When a young woman sitting in a padded chair moved, his eyes settled on her. Beside her chair stood a small circular table with a lantern, a bottle and a glass of wine on it.

The girl turned up the lantern flame and stood.

Tony's jaw dropped and his mouth opened wide enough to halve a peach in one bite. His eyes locked on the face and body of a goddess rising from her throne. *My God, she's beautiful.* A simple form-fitting dress, unbuttoned at the top, fought a hopeless battle to confine her ample breasts and curvaceous body. His mouth clamped shut when Luca spoke.

"You should be asleep by now."

"I wanted to wait," she said.

"This is the American, Tony. Tony, my niece, Anna."

Tony nodded, unable to take his eyes off her. *Gorgeous, but she's maybe sixteen years old.*

Anna reached behind her neck and pulled her long hair over a shoulder, concealing cleavage from Tony's eyes. "It is nice to meet you. You are Italian, from America?"

"Yes, my father grew up near here."

"Welcome to my home."

Tony glanced to the side. Wheels inside his head jumped into high gear. Anna said it was her house. *Luca's dead brother left behind a daughter every man in America would protect with a double barrel shotgun.* "Thank you, miss. I'm here to meet Franco."

She smiled and strolled to him with the precision of an Italian pageant winner.

"Yes, I know why you're here," she said as if the words he muttered were a secret.

His eyes did not leave her and he inhaled when the light scent of her perfume reached the tip of his nose.

Both her hands spread her hair across her breast, concealing them from Tony's eyes. *Stop what's going through your head, she's a young girl.*

Tony slipped a hand behind his back and pinched himself. *I've got a job to do.* "Is he... Franco... is he here?"

"Yes, I will introduce you." She glided across the space between them, stopped and nodded once. "I am Franco," she whispered.

Tony jerked his head back. He did not see that coming and took a double take, twice, between Luca and Anna. "I thought he... I thought Franco was..."

She reached out and touched his arm. "Was a man?"

A rush of heat shot through his body the instant he felt her hand make contact. He nodded before the words reached his lips. "Yes... I... the Germans..."

Anna interrupted. "I know. The Germans also want to meet him."

Luca stepped beside his niece. "My family opposed Fascist violence for many years. We cheered when Mussolini was removed from power. In August, the Allies liberated Sicily, and Anna began helping us fight the Germans. She celebrated her twenty first birthday that month."

Tony's brain had not recovered from the shock. Franklin told him the mission would not be easy, but this made no sense. How could he continue, knowing a young girl who called herself Franco would help him find the Germans? The unfriendly character in the front yard was bad enough, this was nuts.

"What I came here to do will be dangerous. I have to get deep into these mountains and close to the Germans without them seeing me. Your niece is twenty one, but she's still a girl," he said to Luca.

Anna's jaw tightened, and she straightened her shoulders. "We do not plan to die just because you have joined us." She turned her back to him. "You need a glass for wine." She hastened through a doorway.

Luca dropped onto the couch and motioned Tony to join him.

Tony blew air from his lungs and refilled them as he shuffled to the couch and sat beside Luca.

"Don't disregard what Anna says, listen to her. She knows more than you think."

"Why didn't you tell me Franco was a girl?"

"We tell no one, and now you know... you are not to tell anyone."

"Why the name Franco?"

"The Germans have searched for a partisan leader named Franco for the past month. The man is dead... now we play a game. People in the towns tell them peasants led by Franco, a communist leader, are responsible every time we set off a bomb or attack their trucks. Taking the name Franco is her way of defying the Germans. They think of the Amati family as farmers who once made good wine and olive oil."

Tony looked at Anna, sauntering in the room holding two empty glasses. She lifted the wine bottle from the small table, poured and handed a glass to him and her uncle. She eased to the large table against the wall and set the open wine bottle in front of the other four.

"You think I cannot help you?" she asked.

"I have sisters your age. I'm not here to get a young girl killed."

The second the word girl came out of his mouth, Anna's muscles stiffened and she pressed her lips together.

He squirmed in his seat.

Rather than letting it pass, she marched to the couch, planted her feet inches in front of him and locked her dilated eyes on his. "Woman, Tony. Look at me. What you see is a woman."

Damn, what did I say? He turned to Luca.

Luca jumped up and pointed at him. "He cannot stay in the American uniform, Anna. Give him some of your father's clothes."

She replied without turning from Tony. "He can change later."

Luca picked up the carbine. "He can't carry this. I'll give him my gun."

Tony stood and glanced at Luca's submachine gun, leaning against the couch. In Sicily, he had fired one Captain Wilson took off a dead German paratrooper. It packed a lot of firepower.

"Thank you."

"Trust us... trust me," Anna said. She cocked her head to the side and froze at the low sound of an approaching motorcycle.

A sudden coldness shot through Tony's body.

Dario burst into the room. "Two Germans... a sidecar," The door slammed against the frame.

Tony snatched up the MP-40, handed it to Luca, and took the carbine.

Anna grabbed both their wine glasses. "They may have seen or heard the plane. Quick, get everything, go out back!"

Dario led him and Luca through a doorway to the kitchen.

Anna scrambled around the room looking for anything that might show she was not alone. She shoved the two wine glasses behind the couch and set her half-full glass on the small table. As she dropped into the padded chair, she buttoned her dress to the neck. *Why tonight?*

The door swung open and a German sergeant, covered in road dust, stepped into the room. He shut the door, glanced around and smiled when his eyes settled on her. "I saw the light, thought someone was awake. What is your name?"

"Anna." She bit her tongue repressing the hatred he had for all German soldiers. There was no reason to fear him. During the past few weeks, they often came by her house looking for fresh bread, cheese and wine. But never this late.

"I am Otto. You have wine?"

"Yes." Anna stared at him. *The bastard speaks Italian well.*

"Get me a bottle." He plopped on the couch without turning from her.

Anna glanced at the four corked wine bottles on the large table. She left them and lifted the half-full bottle standing in front. *Finish this and go.* She stepped to him and held out the bottle.

"Is anyone else here?"

"No, I'm alone."

"Your husband?"

"I am too young to be married."

He raised the wine bottle to his lips and took a drink. His gaze focused on her eyes, fell to her breasts and stopped at her hips.

Anna avoided eye contact, bit her bottom lip, and inched away.

"Stop."

Tony crouched in the back yard, squeezing his body between a canvas covered donkey cart and the wall of the house. Piles of rusted farm equipment stood near the wall in front and behind him. He took one of his hands from the carbine, pushed the tarp away from his head and scanned the back yard. A large metal washtub sat on a concrete pedestal next to a three-foot high pile of bricks.

He had arrived at the house with Luca less than an hour ago and already found himself in a tight situation. Thinking about the perils of going behind enemy lines and having two Nazi soldiers a few feet away was different. All he could do was hide. His perfect Italian would get him out of trouble, but the American uniform sealed his fate. *Have to get into civvies.*

At the sound of footsteps and the muffled voice of a man humming, he relaxed his muscles and lowered himself closer to the ground. The large canvas provided cover and left him with two small openings so he could see the corner of the house and part of the back yard.

A German private stepped around the corner, strolled to the large tree and looked at the flowers. He lowered his zipper and pissed on the largest bloom. Unarmed except for a dagger hanging from his belt, he had not looked in Tony's direction.

Tony shoved the canvas from the wall for a better view. An empty feeling invaded his stomach when he spotted Dario's boot sticking out from behind the brick pile. The moment Tony looked back at the private, the man's eyes widened, knees bent, and he reached for the handle of his knife. *Damn, we're in trouble. Everyone within a mile will hear a gunshot.*

Tony slowed his breathing, set his carbine on the ground and slid his right hand to the top of his left boot. He hesitated ensuring the German did not see him move and pulled a gold and silver highlighted German SS dagger from its silver inlaid sheath.

The private focused his attention on Dario's boot and crept toward the bricks.

Tony tightened his fingers around the dagger's grip, eased the tarp away from his body and slipped along the wall. When he reached the corner of the house, he stepped behind the soldier. In one swift silent motion, he clamped a hand over the man's mouth and thrust the dagger into his back forcing it into the disc space of his spine. Releasing the knife, he grabbed the soldier's head and snapped his neck.

Anna crossed her arms and froze in front of Otto. She clenched her jaw and stared at him, endeavoring to stop the churning in her stomach. "Take what you want and please leave. It is late."

Otto grinned, exposing teeth caked with wine-stained road dust. "Get another bottle."

She stepped beside the large table and looked at the four bottles of wine. During the next few seconds, thoughts of what she would do raced through her mind. *Will he watch my hands? How fast can I turn... steady myself? How far is the couch?*

"Wait," Otto said.

Her heart jumped in her chest and she quit breathing. She shut her eyes, paused, and filled her lungs with air.

"Bring all of them and take off your dress."

Anna eased air from her expanded lungs and coupled her hands together to stop the trembling. *Relax.* She reached for the bottles with both hands. Her left hand lifted one; the right hand veered behind the others and raised a short barrel German Luger with a six-inch long silencer. As soon as she wrapped her fingers around the pistol grip, she whirled and planted her feet. *Three meters.* In less than two seconds, she aimed and fired three muffled shots.

###

Tony bounced off the kitchen doorframe as he ran into the room. "Anna!" The second he saw her every muscle in his body flexed and he leveled the carbine at a German soldier sitting on the couch with his legs crossed.

In her extended right hand, Anna held a Luger, with a fat silencer pointed at the man's chest. Her left hand clutched a bottle of wine at her side. She turned to Tony and raised her eyebrows. "He's dead."

He lowered his rifle and leaned over for a better look. The hole in the German's forehead and two bloody holes in his chest were the only signs the man no longer enjoyed life on earth. Tony raised his head and watched her lower the Luger to her side. "You did that?"

Luca and Dario raced into the room and froze.

Luca gasped, scanned the room and settled on the dead soldier. "What happened?"

Tony stepped beside Anna, took the bottle of wine from her hand and raised it to Luca. "That German met Franco." He noticed Dario's hands shaking.

"The pig comes into my house for my wine... then he wants my dress."

Tony pointed at the Luger. "How did you get his pistol from him?"

Her head tilted, and she squinted. "His pistol?" She raised the Luger. "This belongs to me." Her posture stiffened, and she thrust an index finger at Dario. "You said there were two."

Tony raised a hand. "Yeah, the other one is out back with my dagger in him." He glanced at Dario when he heard the young man shuffle his feet. *Something is wrong. If he bites down any harder, those teeth will crack.*

Luca slipped out of the room.

"I'm impressed with your accuracy," Tony said.

"I practice, often."

Luca returned and handed Tony his dagger. "Fancy knife."

Tony smiled, wiped the blade on his pants and slid the knife into its leather sheath. "German officer in Sicily didn't need it after we met." The smile on his face disappeared when he turned to Dario. Sweat glowed on the young man's cheeks and forehead. *He's gonna lose it. I hope he isn't always this way.*

Luca removed a German dagger from his back waistband. "The guy out back doesn't need this one, I'll keep it."

Dario stepped toward Tony and pointed at him. "This happened because of you!"

So, it's me. He turned to Luca and spoke each word with a low firm voice. "I suggest you talk with him, or I will."

Luca grabbed Dario's arm and pulled him away from Tony. "Don't be foolish."

"Anna could have been hurt," Dario said.

Tony locked his eyes on Dario and tilted his head toward Anna. "Looks as if she can take care of herself. You need to watch what you're doing and not worry about everyone else. That German in the back yard saw your foot sticking out from behind the bricks."

Anna stepped between them, pressed her lips together, and jerked up her arm. "Enough!"

Chapter IV

NIGHT JUMP

Wish Sergeant DeMarco were here, knowing him, he's drinking wine with a bunch of Italians, Lieutenant Sean Kelly thought.

In 1941, he quit his senior year at Notre Dame to join the army. His sole regret was giving up the fullback position on the football team to a sophomore. He had seven jumps from a C-47 and like most of the man on the plane, tonight would be his second leap into combat.

He stood and secured the buckle of his parachute static line to the cable running the length of the plane. The red jump light glowed across his face. Through the open door, the roar of the engines muffled the voices of the men trying to speak.

Kelly looked at the combat ready paratroopers sitting along the sides of the plane. A mixed bunch of veterans, replacements, men and boys sat next to each other. Al

Bertone and John Rivers were the number the one and two troopers closest to the door. The plane's loadmaster yelled into Kelly's ear.

Kelly exhaled. *Please God. No antiaircraft tonight.* He stepped away from the door and faced his men. The battle ready paratroopers locked their wide eyes on him. He shouted and signaled his jump commands.

Raising his hands, palms out at shoulder level, he thrust them toward the men. "Get readyyyy!" he shouted.

The men turned, sat up, and prepared themselves for the next command. He extended his arms, palms down at waist level, turned his hands palm up, and raised them above his head. "Staaand up!"

Each paratrooper carried over a hundred pounds of equipment. They struggled to lift themselves out of their seats and form a single line facing him. He waited for everyone to stop moving and settle into position. Bending his elbows, Kelly raised his hands to shoulder level and formed index finger hooks with both hands. He lifted and lowered his arms in a pumping motion. "Hook uuup!"

Each man snapped his static line to the taught cable.

###

The blast of the wind from the propeller hit Al as he leapt out the door. His body jerked, and he looked at the open parachute above his head. Just past his canopy, he saw other men streaming from the door of the plane.

The low altitude jump, did not give him much time to prepare for the landing. The instant his toes touched the ground; he turned and rolled across the hard soil. Another paratrooper landed next to him, and moaned upon impact.

Al pulled the parachute harness from his body, grabbed his Thompson submachine gun and slung it across his chest. Distant explosions lit the sky enough for him to see other men landing in the field. He ran past them and found Lieutenant Kelly, the last man out of the C-47.

"Ya okay, sir?"

"Yeah Al." he pointed to the edge of a lemon grove. "Get everyone into those trees and set up defensive positions."

"Ya got it, sir." Al took off into the woods. He spotted Rivers standing motionless in front of a tree surrounded by thick brush. "Rivers, get ya ass over here." The flash of distant explosions provided enough light for him to make out Rivers' face. The young soldier, with wide eyes and an open mouth, did not move. *Shit, something is wrong.* Al raised his submachine gun, crept to within five feet of him and stopped. *Might hit my guys.* He lowered the weapon.

Rivers stood three feet from a set of saucer size eyeballs between two massive black horns.

"I wouldn't move real fast if I were you, Rivers."

The young man eased a hand to his back and wiggled his fingers. He lifted a foot, took a step backwards and turned. "Run!" He and Al raced to the safety of a nearby tree.

"Jesus, sarge. That thing didn't look friendly... scared the Sunday sermon outta me."

"What the hell ya tryin to do, piss him off?"

Rivers turned his boyish face toward the animal. "It snuck up on me like a mouth foaming coon wit rabies... I couldn't move. What the hell is it?"

"A watta buffalo. They're too damn big to sneak around. Pay attention to what you're doing. Ya lucky he didn't ram the shit outta ya. Let's go."

They headed toward a machinegun crew digging a foxhole.

"Ya think Sergeant DeMarco is around here," Rivers asked.

"Nah. I'll bet he's eatin a spaghetti dinner cooked by a resistance guy's girlfriend."

Chapter V

IT'S ALL MINE

Tony stepped away from the bed, threw his T-shirt over his shoulder and shoved his legs into the uniform pants. On his way across the room, he frowned and lifted the shirt to his nose. *Two days of sweat.* He threw it to the floor and stepped to an open window overlooking the back yard.

Anna, facing away from the window, stood beside the large metal washtub and unbuttoned the top of her dress letting it rest on her hips. With a cloth, she washed her face and shoulders, and glanced back to see Tony standing in the window. She covered both breasts with her hands and turned. "The water is warm."

Tony ducked.

He walked out the kitchen door wearing the uniform pants, no shirt or shoes, and carrying civilian clothes she had left for him. He looked at Anna's buttoned damp dress clinging to her shoulders and breasts. "Very pretty."

"Do you like the scenery?"

Tony rubbed the stubble on his chin and grinned. "Oh yeah, it's stunning."

Anna swept her arm across the yard. "It is all belongs to me... as far as you can see."

Damn she's smart. That one needs a reply. He pointed to the large tree. "Those flowers aren't as pretty as you."

"They're planted on top of old graves." She slapped the wet cloth across his bare chest. "Wash, change, and come to the kitchen."

Deadly with a pistol, and a sense of humor. Tony kept his eyes on her until she stepped through the kitchen door.

He walked into the kitchen wearing her father's clothes. An espresso pot steamed on a cast iron stove beside a dome bread oven. Anna picked up the pot and poured strong coffee into two small cups beside a loaf of bread, and marmalade in the center of the wooden table.

She slid into a chair. "I made the bread this morning."

Tony sat next to her, tore a piece off the end of the warm loaf and lifted the coffee cup. "Thank you."

"Tonight we'll leave to meet Dario and Gino," Anna said.

"Who's Gino?"

"A family friend who works with Luca. He lives in the mountains near a town named San Mauro. Luca asked him to find the road the Germans are using to bring in supplies."

"What about Dario? I think he has a problem and I'm it."

Anna tilted her head. "Problem? No. Dario's a good man, but worries too much."

"Maybe he doesn't like Americans."

She scrunched her eyebrows and rubbed the middle of her forehead. "He helped the Americans in Salerno and is helping two officers in the mountains."

"Then I guess it's me he doesn't want to help. If it's going to cause problems, I'd rather stay away from him."

Anna clenched her jaw. "Don't say that... he's my cousin!"

Tony blinked twice and shifted in his chair. "Your cousin? I thought..."

"Dario and I were..."

"No, I..." He slid his hand on top of hers. "I owe you an apology."

She allowed her hand to linger under his as he tightened his fingers.

"Last night you were angry. I shouldn't have called you a girl."

Anna pulled her hand from under his and picked up her cup. "Italian men all want women to stay home and cook." She tried to suppress her smile. "You know I can help."

He looked away and focused on the floor. "Yeah, now I know, but why the hell couldn't I say it?"

"Tu sei italiano. Do you understand?"

"Yes, I am Italian." He stared at the coffee cup and bit his lip.

"What's wrong?"

"Just thinking."

"About what?"

"The men of my platoon jumped in last night. A lot of them may die."

Chapter VI

THE FRONT LINES

Sergeant Bertone crouched behind a tree with Corporals Wolffoot and Thunder, both Cherokee Indians. He pointed at a bomb crater. "Follow me, zig-zag." Al jumped up and crouch-ran toward it. A sound, similar to an electric saw, screamed from a nearby foxhole. Bullets from a German machine gun dug up dirt around his feet as he dove into the large hole in the ground. Seconds later Wolffoot and Thunder landed beside him.

He glanced at the two Indians and grinned. From the first day they arrived in North Africa as replacements, he knew they would fit in well with the other men in the platoon. Every time he called their names he chuckled, and they got fighting mad. He convinced both men that if they had nicknames, no one would laugh when someone called them. On that day, they became Paws and Boom.

Al pulled the shoulder strap of his Thompson over his head. "That's 'Hitler's Buzzsaw'... fucker is fast, I'm glad they can't aim. Both of you get grenades." He raised his submachine gun. "I'll keep their heads down, you guys crawl close enough to drop them on that gun."

Paws and Boom snatched grenades from their belt, slung the M1 rifles over their shoulders, and crept through dried dirt until they were beside Al at the edge of the crater.

"Make sure you keep their heads down," Boom said, to Al.

Paws turned wide eyes and nodded. "Yeah, and ya better get help from the other guys."

"I will. Whatever ya do, don't put your asses in the air." Al shoved the muzzle of his Thompson to the top of the crater and aimed down the barrel. "Cover fire!" He pulled the trigger and fired consecutive three round bursts, and paratroopers on either side of the crater opened up on the enemy machine gun.

Paws and Boom pushed themselves over the edge of the hole and crawled toward the German machine gun nest. Paratroopers, hidden in positions near the crater, kept firing, forcing the enemy gunners to seek cover. The two Indians crawled within thirty feet of the Nazi position and lobbed the grenades. Explosions silenced the enemy weapon.

Lieutenant Kelly ran past the crater and took cover behind a tree. Al jumped from the shallow pit and ran to him. Captain Wilson and a radio operator joined them. All three men saw blood on Kelly's arm.

"You okay?" Wilson asked.

"Yeah, only a scratch."

Al wiped perspiration from his forehead and eyes. When he looked at his hand, he cringed at the sight of blood. "Damn."

Kelly glanced at him and shuffled back a step. "Christ Bertone, get back to a medic."

"It's nutin, sir." He slid his fingers across his soaked forehead.

"Get going, sergeant," Wilson ordered.

Al carried his helmet and pressed his bare hand against his forehead while he trudged toward the company medics tending to the wounded.

Doc, his platoon medic, jumped up with a hand full of gauze. "Let me see that."

Al wiped his hand across the gash, smearing blood across his face.

Doc slapped his hand from his head. "Why don't you just wipe shit in it, you wanna infection? Where's your sulfa pack?"

Al reached for a small pouch attached to his belt. "Right here."

"Keep it in case you need it later, I've got a can full." Doc sprinkled sulfur powder on gauze he had folded into a compress and swiped it across the wound.

"Jesus, ya tryin-ah kill me?"

Doc shook his head and rolled his eyes. He held up the bloody dressing. "Yeah, I'm gonna rub you to death with this." He pressed it against the cut with his thumbs.

"Damn!" Suddenly light-headed, Al swayed and his eyes rolled back.

Doc grabbed him. "You all right?"

"Yeah, I think so."

"You puke on me, I'm gonna stitch up your head with parachute cord, you'll look like that Frankenstein guy in the movie." Doc handed him a handful of clean gauze. "Keep pressure on it."

He pressed the fabric against his wound and watched Doc walk away. Thoughts of the day he entered the Army flashed through his mind. A sergeant asked him if he wanted to become a medic and carry an aid-kit instead of a rifle. War without a gun didn't make sense to him. Patching up holes in people was more difficult than putting holes in them. He pressed the gauze against his forehead. *Thank God someone wants to do it.*

Al spotted Rivers shuffling toward him. The young soldier clamped his teeth on his lip and held his left hand in a blood soaked pocket. "What the hell happened?"

"Cut my hand."

"Lotta damn blood for a cut. Let me see it."

Rivers held his pocket open with his right hand. He cringed as he lifted his left hand and extended his open palm.

A small stump stuck out where his little finger should have been. Blood dripped to the ground.

"That's ya Purple Heart, kid."

"Rather have my finger back."

Doc squeezed between Al and Rivers. He grabbed Rivers' hand, examined the tiny red stump and grinned. He tipped the can and poured sulfur on the wound. "Give him a piece of your gauze."

Al pulled the compress from his head and stared at it. "It's bloody."

"So is his hand." Doc walked away.

He ripped off a small strip of bandage that remained somewhat white and handed it to Rivers. "Sergeant DeMarco didn't want you to get hurt, he's gonna be pissed."

VII

MOUNTAINSIDE

Tony walked out the kitchen door carrying two German submachine guns and a civilian backpack.

Light flashed in the night sky followed by the distant rumble of battle.

Anna, wearing pants, a man's shirt and boots, stood beside a small gray donkey hooked to a cart. A knit bag hung from her shoulder and a large canvas bag and backpack lay on the ground near her feet. She rubbed her hand across the donkey's neck. "This is Peppino."

Tony grinned.

"The clothes fit you quite well." She lifted the pack and canvas bag by their straps and dropped them on a tarp behind the cart seat. "Put the guns in the back and cover everything."

Tony pointed at the large canvas bag. "What's in that?"

"Bread, cheese, sausage and wine. Italians need to eat."

"You don't forget anything, do you?"

Anna tilted her head and pursed his lips. "I have done this before... remember?"

During the next two hours, Anna guided the donkey cart through trees as they headed uphill. Tony sat quietly beside her, watched her tap Peppino's back with a long stick and adjust the knit bag hanging from her shoulder. *She knows what she is doing.*

"Do you have children?" she asked.

"No wife, no kids, only the army."

"Who is in Ponte?"

"Six of my uncles and four aunts."

"It's near here."

Tony nodded.

"Will you visit them?"

The thought never left his mind. "If this war lets me."

Without looking at him, Anna touched his arm and did not remove her hand. "Take me when you go."

Less than twenty-four hours ago Tony stepped into Anna's house and in that time his feelings for her had changed. When he first saw her, he thought she was a teenager and wondered how the war must horrify her. It did not take long for him to realize she was a perceptive resistance fighter, who happened to be a knockout. He placed his hand over hers and stared at her until she looked into his eyes. "I've never met anyone like you."

Anna turned her head, slipped her hand from his and pointed to the right. "We're almost there. We need to go that way."

"How do you know? The trees all look the same."

"Do you remember the streets where you live?"

"Sure I do."

"All of them?"

"Almost all."

She lifted her shoulders and raised her hands. "Here we have few streets, but I know all the trees."

Within five minutes, they came upon Dario, sitting under a tree with a rope tied around the base. His rifle lay at his side and a backpack and bucket of water sat near the tree.

Anna stopped Peppino beside him.

Tony grabbed her backpack and canvas bag from behind the seat and hopped from the cart. He threw his backpack over his shoulder, slid the two submachine guns from under the tarp and handed one of the weapons to Anna.

Dario unhooked the donkey, tied him to the tree and slid the bucket to him.

"Here, Dario." She adjusted the knit bag over her shoulder and handed the submachine gun to him. "This is for you. The magazines are in the canvas bag."

Dario examined the weapon and smiled. "Thank you." He tossed his old rifle into the cart, picked up his backpack and motioned for them to follow.

"Where's Gino?" Tony asked.

"You will meet him tomorrow. The two American officers are nearby." Dario headed through the trees.

Chapter VIII

THE WOODEN HOUSE

Second Lieutenant Mike Kramer, a pilot, and Second Lieutenant Jack Stevens, an infantry platoon leader, sat on large rocks inside the dilapidated wooden and stone house on the side of the mountain. The two officers heated canned rations over a small fire in a hole they dug in the dirt floor. The structure provided cover for the two men and their jeep.

I'll never volunteer again. Kramer thought. "You know anything about the sergeant that's coming here?"

"Just that he's a paratrooper."

"I'll bet he volunteered like we did. An eight ball looking for a stripe."

Stevens stuck his Kabar knife into a small open can and stirred bubbling franks and beans. "The Italian guy said a colonel picked him for the job."

"I'll stake you the next bottle of whiskey I buy... if we ever get out of this place, that he was the colonel's jeep driver."

When they heard a single knock and a board creak, they turned their heads toward the sound.

"Dario's back," Stevens said.

Dario, Tony and Anna approached the two young officers. *This is a shit hole,* Tony thought.

Anna set the canvas bag on the dirt floor.

Kramer and Stevens, with their mouths hanging open, looked at her as if she were Jane Russell stepping out of a pin-up photo in Yank magazine, and then grinned.

"Nice," Kramer said.

"Who's the pretty broad?" asked Stevens.

They jumped to their feet.

"Would you like a ride in my airplane? What's your name beautiful?" Kramer asked.

Tony swallowed hard, muscles and veins strained against his skin. *They think they hit the jackpot.* He reached into Anna's canvas bag and removed a sausage.

Stevens looked past them at the hole in the wall where they entered. "Where's the paratrooper?"

Tony bent forward and removed the knife from his leg sheath. He straightened his frame, and stared into the lieutenant's eyes, focused on the German dagger. With his knife, he cut two pieces of sausage and stabbed one, impaling it on the tip of the blade. The first piece he handed to Kramer and then swung the knife toward Stevens. The lieutenant's gaze did not stray from him while removing the piece of meat from the tip of the weapon.

"I'm Staff Sergeant Antonio DeMarco."

Kramer stopped chewing and swallowed twice. "We thought you were Italian."

"I am, lieutenant."

"Sorry. I meant you were just... just an Italian."

"The Army made you both officers and gentlemen?" Tony didn't wait for an answer. "My family lives in Italy." He took a deep breath to calm himself. *I'll end this now.* He reached for Anna's hand. "This is my cousin, Anna." The dagger, in his right hand, rested against his chest, with the point inches below his chin. "Do not speak to her that way again. You both may think you are invincible, but any night of the week, a German could sneak in here and slit your throats." Tony tapped the dagger against his chest. "And if, for an unknown reason, a German eighty-eight gun crew found out you were camping in this dump, they might put it on their target practice list." He slid the dagger into its sheath.

"We're sorry. It's been hell here," Stevens said. "We've had to hide and watch the fight in the valley."

"Watch the fight?" Tony shook his head. "I fought my way through North Africa and jumped into Sicily to kick German asses. Been shot at and missed, and shit at and hit. Last night I parachuted in, came all the way up here, and find two lieutenants watching the war."

Dario opened his backpack and passed two loaves of bread and two sausages to Kramer.

Anna whispered to him and handed him the canvas bag.

He removed a bottle of wine and gave it to Stevens.

The lieutenant looked at her with a sheepish expression. "Thank you, miss."

Both of the officers avoided eye contact with Tony. The tension in the room settled and everyone relaxed.

"Did they brief you on why I'm here?" Tony asked.

Kramer nodded.

"If I can find which mountain pass the Germans are using, I'll call for planes. It's your job to make sure I get them."

Kramer looked at him and shook his head. "That may be a problem... not much air support the last two days."

"There will be. The brass figured out the 36th Infantry is getting the shit kicked out of them. They may lose this battle." Tony gestured toward Dario. "He'll stay here with you, any questions?"

Stevens glanced at Kramer and turned to Tony. "No."

"If the Germans spot you, he's the guy who can get you out. Treat him right."

"We will," both replied in unison.

Tony removed a map from his backpack and waved it. "There's a lot to cover, we need to sit down and take a look at this."

An hour later, Tony, Anna and Dario walked toward the donkey cart.

Perfect time to talk to him. Tony tapped Dario on the shoulder and they stopped. "We'll be there in a minute," he said to Anna and watched her continue through the trees.

"Those two don't know it's dangerous in these mountains. Keep them out of trouble. Without you, they'll get their asses captured."

"I will."

"Anna told me you know where to meet us."

"Yes."

"Make sure you get there on time."

"Don't worry about me, I will be. Make sure you're there with my cousin."

Tony shut his eyes for a few seconds and stopped breathing. Anna was not with them and Dario had no reason to act like a big shot. "I know you don't like me, but we need to work together."

Dario stared into his eyes. "I don't want Anna hurt."

"That won't happen. I'll never..."

"When you leave us, you'll go back to America." Dario inched closer.

"When the war is over I will, but I won't hurt Anna."

Dario shoved his index finger into Tony's chest. "If you do..."

Blood pounded in Tony's head. Without thinking about the consequences of his actions, he widened his stance, and grabbed Dario's wrist. With little effort, he spun him around and pinned his arm to his back. Tony's free hand clamped around Dario's neck.

Anna dashed to Tony's side. "Tony, stop!" She pulled his hand away from Dario's throat. She glared at both men and her voice shook when she spoke. "Are you both crazy?"

"Your cousin needs to know if he threatens someone, he may have to kill him," Tony said.

Anna pulled Dario by the arm. "Why are you doing this?"

"He'll break your heart."

Hands trembling at her side, she paused on each word. "I am not a child."

"You're still a girl," Dario said.

The second she heard the word girl, she stepped back and looked at both men. Her eyes filled with tears. "Italian men. Both of you look at me. Do you see a school girl in a dress?" She turned tearful eyes to Tony. "Do you?"

Tony shook his head. "No." A moment earlier, he said he would do nothing to harm her, and when he grabbed Dario, he had made her angry.

She glared at Dario and waited for his response.

"No," he said.

"Apologize." She wiped her tears, waited a moment and placed her hands on her hips. "Now, or you both can go to hell."

Tony extended his hand. "I'm sorry."

"I apologize." Dario lowered his head. "He comes here and gives orders."

"The Americans gave him a job to do." Anna said.

"We're family, Anna."

She pointed at Tony. "His family is nearby."

"That's different."

"No, Dario. You don't see it, but I'm different. Tony doesn't make me feel like a child, he treats me like a woman... not the girl you see."

Dario's shoulders drooped, and he tilted his head. "I'm sorry. I worry about you."

"Then you need to help Tony... help me."

She stepped beside Tony. "I'm ready to go."

While they walked to the cart, Tony berated himself for what he had done to Dario. He tapped the young man on the arm. "Don't worry, I promise she'll be safe."

Tony transferred food from the canvas bag to his backpack and threw it over his shoulders. He motioned to the knit tote hanging over Anna's shoulder. "What's in that?"

Anna removed the bag and pulled out the silenced Luger. "Protection from German and Italian men." She replaced the pistol and hung the bag from her shoulder. "We need to leave."

Chapter IX

THE TOMB

Tony and Anna kept conversation to a minimum while they trudged through moonlit trees along the edge of a four-foot wide mountain stream. Set back from the opposite bank, thick vines covered a fifteen-foot high stone wall.

Anna slowed and studied the vines. "We'll stop up there, on the other side of the stream."

He scanned the terrain on either side of the creek. "Where? Didn't you say we'd be hidden?"

"I did, come."

They continued a short distance along the stream and Anna stopped at the edge of the water. She pointed at the mass of vines clinging to the stone. "Do you see it?"

Tony studied the thick vegetation crawling to the top of the wall. *Yeah, plants clinging to stone.* He shook his head.

Anna took his hand and led him across the stream. She parted a section of the vines to expose a hole, large enough for a person to enter. Removing a candle and a tin of matches from her knit bag, she lit the candle and crawled in the hole.

Tony followed her into the cave and looked around the cavern carved into stone. Cut into the rock, along the sidewalls, were solid stone benches. A lantern sat on the bench closest to Anna.

She lit the lantern.

"God, how old is this place?"

"Almost two thousand years old, it's a Roman tomb."

Tony set his pack and weapon down and walked to a canvas, partially covering German wooden ammo crates, at the back of the cave. He removed the canvas and opened a crate. Blankets, pots, cups, towels and cans of lamp oil filled the box. The thought of standing in a tomb amazed him and he scanned the chamber. *People back home say Boston is old. I'm standing in the middle of a tomb, built by men over a thousand years before anyone knew America existed.* The hairs on his arms stood on end. "Once the grave of a Roman... now it serves as a partisan hiding place. Do you know who was buried here?"

"No."

Anna took blankets from the crate and laid them on the floor. She sat on a blanket, removed food and wine from Tony's backpack, and pulled out a red canvas panel. "What is this?"

"Half of a panel to mark the ground for paratroopers. They jump from the plane when it passes over the marker."

Anna shrugged and stuffed it back into the pack. "Let's eat."

Tony sat beside her and poured wine into two cups.

"How did you know your family lives in Ponte?" she asked.

"I've known since I was a child. My father spoke of them often. When I said I would fight the Germans, he told me to make sure I visited my aunts and uncles."

"Did he know you would come here?"

Tony smiled and shook his head. "No. Italy sided with the Germans but the Italians in America didn't. He figured the war would end much sooner." He studied her as she sipped wine. "Tell me about your parents."

She pulled a finger-full of hair over her shoulder, tilted her head and chewed on the hair between her fingers. "Seven years ago my mother died."

"Sorry."

Anna looked at him and a tear rolled down her cheek. "The Fascists killed my father. Once the news of Mussolini's defeat in Greece and Egypt became known, he protested against Italy's 'Pact of Steel' with Germany. The 'Black Shirts' assassinated him and two of his friends." She raised her head, wiped the tear and her eyes brightened. "I have a sister named Bianca. She is a year younger... we look like twins."

"Where is she now?"

"Uncle Luca sent her south to a small town in Calabria."

"When is she coming back?"

"Soon I hope."

Anna shoved herself from the blanket and picked up a large copper pot near the crates.

Tony rolled to his knees as she approached the entrance. Thoughts of the worst-case scenario flashed through his mind. *What if someone sees her crawling out the hole?* He raised a hand. "Where are you going?"

"To get water."

"Are you sure it's safe?"

Anna waved a hand at him. "Only my family knows this place. When I was a child, my mother and father brought my cousin and me up this mountain. Dario pressed a stick against the rock wall while he ran along the stream. When the stick came to this hole, he lost his balance and fell into the water." Tears formed in the corners of her eyes. "Father always said this place was our secret."

"And now... my secret."

Anna nodded and went out the hole.

Tony opened his backpack and removed an Army radio. He rubbed dust from the small transceiver, checked for damage and returned it to his pack.

Anna crawled through the opening shoving the full pot of water in front of her. She carried it to the back wall.

"If we were not in the middle of a war, with Germans all around us, we could visit my family," Tony said.

"One day we will."

Tony's heart fluttered. *Yes. We will.* He watched Anna remove a cloth from a crate, turn away and lower her shirt. She washed her upper body, raised her shirt and secured the buttons.

"There's enough water left for you." She pulled a dry cloth from a crate, sat on the blanket and wiped her face.

Tony headed to the back wall. After he washed, he removed another blanket. "We need to get a little rest."

"I'll empty the pot." She approached the cave entrance and froze. "Someone is coming." She scrambled away from the hole and blew out the lantern.

Tony grabbed his weapon and Anna her knit bag. Both crawled to the entrance. He reached out and adjusted the vines to better conceal the opening. Both peered through the spaces between leaves.

Tony raised his head and looked over his shoulder. He crinkled his nose. "Oil."

Thirty feet from the hole, he saw four German soldiers, led by a young private.

Seventeen-year-old Jarvis Becka, the youngest of the four German soldiers, led the patrol along the stream descending the hillside. None of the others, including Sergeant Hans Dott, the patrol leader, concerned themselves with remaining quiet. Hans told him the Americans could not get off the beach and the patrol would be fifteen kilometers from the nearest British or American unit. *I need a cigarette.*

He stopped near a tree and raised an arm to Hans. "We should stop here and fill our canteens."

Hans nodded and turned to the two men behind him. "Rest for fifteen minutes, get water if you need it." No one hesitated. They dropped to the ground, set down their weapons and removed their packs.

Jarvis raised his canteen to his lips and drained it, sucking out the last few drops of water. From his pocket, he pulled a crumbled pack of cigarettes. *No telling when we will stop again.* He climbed to his feet, lit a cigarette and strolled toward the stream. When he reached the edge of the water, he squatted, set his cigarette next to his boot and tilted his canteen, placing it below the surface. Jarvis focused on bubbles flowing from the opening as it filled. The vines and trees along the stream drew his attention. He frowned, leaned his head back, and sucked air into his nostrils.

"Hans." Jarvis stood and looked toward the sergeant.

Hans could be grumpy, but he always treated his men well. When others spoke of the war, or of Adolf Hitler, he never smiled. Jarvis did not care if he ever saw a British or American soldier or if he ever fired his rifle. He hoped Hans felt the same way.

Hans trudged to the creek and stepped beside him. "What?"

Jarvis squinted, turned his head and sniffed the air. "Oil. I smell oil burning."

Hans took a breath through his nose. His forehead furrowed, and he sniffed two more times. "Are you sure?"

"I don't know."

Hans turned, raised his head and scrunched his eyes. A wisp of smoke passed his face, and he looked at the ground. The cigarette smoldered in the dry brush between him and Jarvis. He stomped on the cigarette and turned a 'maybe I will kill you' look at Jarvis. Hans pulled the young soldier away from the stream. "Dumb ass."

They marched to the other men.

"Get up... we are leaving!" Hans said.

Tony slid from the tomb opening and lit the lantern. "Luck of the Irish."

Anna scratched her cheek. "The Irish? They were Germans."

He grinned with his mouth shut to keep from laughing. "It's an American saying."

"I don't understand."

He tickled her until she squirmed. "I'll teach you."

They dropped to the blanket and faced each other.

"Let's get three or four hours sleep," Tony said.

Anna slid her body against his and placed her head on his chest. "I cannot sleep tonight."

Just a dumb thought I had. Tony winked at her. "The lantern," he whispered.

Chapter X

WE'RE LOST

After sunrise, Tony and Anna remained alert while they moved through the trees heading deeper into the mountains. The trip was not a constant uphill climb. An hour earlier, they crossed a saddle between two hills.

In an area of dense forest, a middle-aged man in civilian clothes and a canvas bag hanging from his shoulder, stepped from behind a tree. "Anna," he called.

Tony turned his submachine gun toward the man.

Anna grabbed Tony's arm, "It's Gino."

Gino walked to them nodding. "You don't look like an American but you must be Tony." He kissed Anna's cheek.

"How'd you know my name?" Tony asked.

"Among our group, news travels fast in these mountains."

Anna helped Tony remove his pack. She sat and opened it.

"Where's your weapon?" Tony asked.

Gino looked at him with a twinkle of mischief in his eyes. "I can explain why I'm here." He removed a large mushroom from the pouch and held it out to Tony. "If the Germans found me with a gun, they would not listen to what I had to say. Mushrooms, they understand."

"I think I'll take my chances," Tony said.

They joined Anna on the ground.

"An hour from here, the Germans are gathering supplies and bringing in more men," Gino said.

"Where?"

"Along a valley road, between the mountains. It's a large camp... fuel barrels, ammunition and during the past two days, I've seen tanks."

Anna handed Gino a bottle of wine and Tony bread.

"Can we get near it?" Tony asked

"We need to wait until tonight, during the day is too dangerous."

Anna held up a sausage. Tony slid his dagger from its sheath and handed it to her. She cut the sausage, handed pieces to both men and gave Tony the dagger.

Gino's mouth slackened. He shook his head and pointed at the knife. "If the Germans see that, you will die. There will be no questions."

Tony slid the dagger into its sheath. "I have no plans to show it to them."

Well after midnight, Tony heard the hum of generators as Gino led him and Anna toward the edge of a dirt road.

Throughout his five years in the army, he had led quite a few patrols. During the long walk from where they first met, Gino impressed him, saying they needed to stay quiet. They avoided areas of little concealment, even when it meant taking a longer route. *He's better at this than I thought.*

An hour later they had approached a dirt road and concealed themselves in the underbrush.

Tony could not count the number of light bulbs hanging from wires strung between poles. He pointed at them and whispered to Gino. "It's lit-up like a city street. They must not be worried about an attack."

"We're almost twenty kilometers from the American positions and even further from the British. There is no reason to hide."

Tony surveyed the depot. Across from where they hid, a large tent stood to the side of storage areas separated by low barbwire fences. Stacked barrels of fuel bordered the far side of the tent. A dirt road cut in front of the tent, separating it and the barrels from stacked wooden crates of ammunition.

Gino pointed at the tent and a light/truck staff car parked in front. "The car is for the senior officer. Soldiers are in the tent day and night. It's the command center." He motioned to a parking area across from the tent. "Yesterday, four tanks stopped there for fuel."

"I need to get closer, you and Anna stay here," Tony said.

Anna grabbed his arm. "You can't."

He patted her hand. "Don't worry, wait here, I'll be back in a few minutes."

Colonel Eric Mayer shoved aside a canvas dividing the tent into two distinct parts. He stepped into the command center section. Empty chairs sat in front of tables covered with field telephones, maps, radios and typewriters. Mayer smiled at a soldier occupying a single chair in front of a large radio atop a table against the tent wall. The radio operator leapt to his feet and snatched the headphones from his ears.

"Is it quiet tonight, corporal?" Mayer asked.

"Yes, sir, everyone in Berlin must be asleep."

"They sleep, we work." Mayer shoved the canvas aside and entered his private living quarters on the other side of the tarp. *We fight the war... they drink schnapps and sleep in feather beds.*

The accommodations were not much for an officer of his rank, but he remained satisfied with what he had. The small comfortable bed and the wooden box beside it, serving as a bedside table, met his needs. He spent most of his time at the two tables his men made into a desk, befitting a senior officer and veteran of the first war.

Mayer tightened the light bulb hanging above his desk and dropped into the chair. This time at night, he knew no one would call; he slid the field telephone from the center of the desk. Mayer shifted his shoulders and pulled on the suspenders, digging into his T-shirt. He glanced at his favorite seat. A month ago, he liberated the oversized padded armchair from a villa outside Naples.

"Colonel Mayer." The canvas parted and Lieutenant David Schmitz stepped into the room.

Mayer pressed his lips together. Schmitz performed his duties well as his aid, but he took a little too much interest in the Aryan master race and the writings of Günther in his book *Racial Science of the German People.*

"Yes, come in, Schmitz."

He marched to the desk and snapped to attention. Dust covering his form fitting uniform jumped from the fabric and floated to the desk.

Mayer frowned. *Impressive military bearing, but useless in battle.*

"I spoke with a tank commander. Tiger tanks will arrive in the morning, sir," Schmitz said.

"Part of the Herman Goering Division?"

"Yes, sir, but we have a problem."

"A small one I hope."

Schmitz shrugged his shoulders. "We have enough fuel for one day."

Mayer slammed a hand on the desk. A sour taste filled his mouth. He needed to spit and swallowed. "Goering's panzers... he is a Reichsmarschall, Hitler's successor, he can't be that stupid. Petrol needs to go with the tanks."

"Sir, Herr Goering is not with them, he's in Berlin."

"His fat ass should be here, Schmitz. Not in a whorehouse playing with the portly ladies who want entry to the Reich Chancellery." Mayer sprang to his feet. "Contact headquarters... get someone in Berlin out of bed. Panzers without fuel are useless."

Schmitz snapped to attention, clicked his heels and thrust an arm forward. "Heil Hitler."

Mayer's nostrils flared, his face reddened.

Schmitz dropped his arm.

Mayer pushed away from the desk and dropped into his favorite seat. He adjusted himself and lifted his head to the lieutenant. "The little illegitimate Austrian cannot help us, Schmitz. He is busy licking his wounds from Stalingrad and running west, away from Ivan."

"Sir the fuhrer..."

Mayer lifted his hand to stop him. "Do you want to win this war or please him?"

Anna and Gino watched Tony's faint image dash from boulder to boulder at the rear of the tent.

Gino leaned to her. "Come on, be quiet." He and Anna crept through the trees along the edge of the road.

The butt of a rifle slammed into Gino's back, knocking him to the ground.

Anna turned and froze. The sound of her heartbeat pounded in her ears. Her eyes, inches from the muzzle of a submachine gun, bulged, legs weakened. The instant she saw the two German soldiers, she tightened her lips to keep them from trembling. The tall man, closest to her, lowered the barrel of his MP-40 to her chest.

Gino rolled onto his back and held his hands in front of his body when he saw a short, overweight, soldier standing over him pointing a rifle at his head.

Anna's pulse raced. She gathered as much information as possible while she watched the two Germans. Her mind focused on finding a way out of the situation. *The one with the submachine gun may be in charge. The little fat one, with the maniacal eyes, scares me.*

"Hello, frauline. My name is Günter." He pointed at the little fat man. "He is Claus."

Anna turned her head from side to side. *Find a way out.* "We're lost."

"Lost? Where are you going?" Günter asked.

Claus kicked Gino. "Get up!"

Before she could say anything in her defense, Günter pulled Anna's pack from her back and snatched the bag from her shoulder. He shoved a hand into the knit bag and glared at her as he removed the Luger with the silencer screwed onto the barrel. With his hand around the pistol grip, he placed his finger on the trigger. "Do all lost girls in Italy carry a Gestapo pistol?"

The fat soldiers' chilling eyes locked on the pistol as if he had never heard the word Gestapo or seen a silencer. He glanced at her and then back to the weapon.

It took Gino less than a second to react. He lunged at Claus' rifle.

Günter stepped back and fired two muffled shots into Gino's chest.

Anna rocked in place and gasped. She held back a scream, leaned and reached for Gino.

The side of Claus' rifle slammed into her ribs.

She stumbled, regained her footing and focused on the Luger, two inches from her forehead. Tears slid down her cheeks and she stepped back, avoiding eye contact with Günter or the pistol. Her mouth became dry and the possibility of death flashed into her thoughts.

"Come with us and be quiet or I'll let Claus kill you."

Claus shoved Anna toward the road. He planted the muzzle of his weapon in the middle of her back and nudged her forward.

Anna glanced toward the tent. *Where is Tony?*

Tony dashed behind a large boulder and peered around it. Movement drew his eyes to the road, and he watched three dark figures heading towards the front of the tent. The instant they passed under a light, every muscle in his body tightened and the hair on the nape of his neck stiffened. Two German soldiers forced Anna toward the tent. *Maybe Gino got away. I need to do something.* He took a single step away from his concealed position but stopped and scooted back behind the rock. Several irrational plans bounced around inside his head, but he knew he could do nothing but watch. Any action he took would turn into a disaster, compounding their problems and making it more dangerous for them both. He bit his lip and watched.

The short soldier shoved the muzzle of his rifle into Anna's back and she fell to her knees.

Tony steadied himself against the rock and raised his MP-40. Squeezing the pistol grip and the upper part of the magazine, he took aim. The soldier yanked Anna to her feet and stepped beside her, blocking Tony's line of sight. Ordering himself to calm down, he relaxed his grip on the weapon. *I'll end up getting us both killed.* He removed his backpack and opened it.

Dim light illuminated Mayer, reclining on his bed and staring at the top of the tent post. His suspenders, cast off his shoulders, hung at his waist.

The Allied foothold on the Italian coast at Salerno seldom left his thoughts. One day he hoped to return to his wife and children in the small town of Brunnthal, south of Munich. Unless the high command in Berlin took the loss of Sicily more seriously, and the landing at Salerno with a sense of urgency, that day may not come. *The General Staff should listen to the commanders at the front, not the little corporal, Hitler.*

"Sir, are you awake?" Schmitz asked, from the other side of the canvas.

"Yes, Schmitz." Mayer swung his feet to the floor and walked to his desk.

The lieutenant stopped in front of the desk and snapped an arm salute. "Heil, Hitler."

Mayer shook his head and tightened the light bulb hanging above his desk.

"We captured a girl hiding in the trees near the road," Schmitz said.

"The German army now captures children?"

Schmitz shuffled his feet. "No, sir, a young woman. Concealed in a bag, she had a Luger with a silencer."

Mayer frowned, tightened his jaw and looked down at his desk. *The Gestapo use silencers.* "Have her brought here."

"Yes, sir." Schmitz thrust his arm forward, looked at his commander, and lowered it to his side. He spun around and marched toward the canvas wall.

"Schmitz," Mayer called.

"Yes, Colonel."

"Thank you."

Anna knew she was in serious trouble the minute the Germans killed Gino. She pressed her back against the chair next to the tent pole not far from Mayer's desk and wiped tears and dried sweat from her cheeks. The steel leg iron, clamped around her left ankle and the tent pole, kept her prisoner. Anna stared at the man sitting across from her.

Mayer leaned forward in his comfortable chair. His fingers toyed with the grip of the Luger and he stroked his chin with the forefinger and thumb of his free hand. Günter had brought her into the room five minutes earlier, but the man in the chair had not spoken.

He placed the Luger on the armrest and spoke in a low tone. "I am Colonel Eric Mayer."

Anna nodded. The tightness in her chest slackened. *Thank God. He's a senior officer... more civilized than the two who brought me here.*

Mayer tapped the Luger. "Where did you get this pistol?" His words, spoken in perfect Italian were soft and distinct.

"A German officer gave it to my father."

"Why?"

"He helped him find vegetables and wine for his men."

"When did this happen?"

"A few months ago."

Mayer stared at her and scratched the stubble on his face. "Why do you have it?"

"For protection."

"What was his name?"

"Francesco." Her heart jumped inside her chest the second the words left her lips. She realized her mistake.

"A German officer named Francesco?"

"No, my father."

"You do not know the officer's name, do you?"

Anna shook her head. "I don't remember."

Mayer smiled and slid out of his chair. "I will return. I do not want you to hurt yourself. It would be best if you do not think about trying to escape."

Anna watched Mayer leave. She looked around the tent, taking in each object, piece of furniture, and their positions in the room. She glanced at the clamp around her ankle. Leaning over, she fiddled with the leg iron and attempted to slide her foot from it. *I'm not going anywhere with this on my leg.* The soldier who had clamped and locked the manacle did his job well. She couldn't free herself.

A lieutenant burst into the room and frowned. He marched to Anna's chair, stopped inches in front of her and tapped his chest. "Lieutenant Schmitz. Your name?"

Anna glared at him, trying to understand what he said in crude Italian.

Before she could move, the knuckles on the back of Schmitz's hand slammed against her face. The taste of blood filled her mouth.

"Answer me."

Anna pressed her lips together and glared at him.

He grabbed the front of her shirt and jerked her to her feet. The shirt ripped, exposing part of her breasts. She tightened her hands around the fabric and pressed the pieces together at her neck. *Give me a chance and I'll kill you.*

Schmitz drew his Luger, placed the muzzle against her forehead and spoke slowly. She understood the words, 'I... not ask... again'.

Anna looked into his eyes. *You arrogant bastard.* "Anna," she whispered.

"Your surname?"

"Bianco."

He re-holstered the pistol. "Where do you live?"

"In Eboli."

Schmitz looked at her ripped shirt and hands holding it against her breasts. He pulled her hands down to her waist and glared at her breasts.

Anna's eyes widened and blood drained from her face. She held her breath.

The instant she heard someone yell "Schmitz", she and the lieutenant turned to the canvas separating the two sections of the tent.

Colonel Mayer stood holding her Luger at his side. His wide eyes, contorted face and stiff posture radiated anger.

Schmitz stepped back.

He and the colonel shouted in German, and she understood an occasional word.

The lieutenant did not move when Mayer shouted and swept his arm toward the canvas wall.

She grabbed the fabric of her torn shirt, lifted it, and held the two pieces together. *They'll take out their anger on me.*

Schmitz said something, and she caught one word, "Gestapo".

Mayer's face reddened and when he spoke, she recognized the words, "I do not" and "fuhrer".

The young officer glared at Mayer, yelled, and started toward him.

"Nein," Mayer said, as he raised the Luger and fired two shots into his lieutenant's chest.

Schmitz crumbled to the floor in front of Anna.

Mayer set the pistol beside the field telephone on his desk, walked to the overstuffed armchair and dropped into it. He shook his head and spoke to her in Italian. "The Nazis will kill us all. I will say you killed him."

Anna watched blood pool on the floor beside the dead man's body. *I can't believe he shot him. He must not be a Nazi. It's my only chance.*

Her eyes remained on the lieutenant while she spoke to Mayer. "If you say I killed him, they'll kill me."

"I will not let that happen."

Anna lifted her head, her eyes brightened, and she grinned. "You have no choice. Let me escape or you'll die."

Mayer shifted, rocking from side to side in the chair. "You are in my tent, surrounded by my men. To suggest that you can leave here, or I will die, is foolish."

Anna smiled at him. "No, I'm not a fool. I need to leave, now. After what you did, I know you don't want to harm me, and I don't want to harm you."

"What is your name?"

"Anna."

"Well, my child, I may help you and keep you alive, but escape is out of the question. Too many people know

Günter brought you here and they will ask questions. I am sorry. Freedom is not possible."

The blade of a gold and silver inlayed dagger came to rest against the skin of Mayer's neck. His eyes bulged, and he stopped breathing.

"You are wrong, Colonel. Freedom is possible, my men are nearby," Tony said. "I believe you're a gentleman. If you remain quiet, I'll let you live. If not, you'll die without making a sound."

Mayer froze in his chair and locked his large eyes on Anna.

Chapter XI

MOVING OUT

Sergeant Bertone sat with a group of exhausted and dirty paratroopers, in positions among the trees. During the lull in fighting, each man remained alert to the distant sounds of planes, bombs and artillery explosions. Al often stressed to them that a lackadaisical attitude brought death closer to their doorstep.

Lieutenant Sean Kelly sat at the edge of the group and did not notice Captain Wilson approaching.

"Get'em ready, Sean, we're moving out."

"Where we headed, sir?" Al yelled.

"Northeast, leg infantry will take over these positions," Wilson said.

Kelly pushed himself from the ground and moaned as he stood.

Al respected the lieutenant. *He's as tired and sore as we are.* During his time in the army, Al served with many officers who kept the men under their command at a safe distance. Kelly wasn't that type of man. If his men rolled in shit, he came out stinking, just as much as they did.

"How long before we leave," Kelly asked.

"Couple of hours." Wilson pointed over his shoulder. "There's hot chow two hundred yards back."

Infantry soldiers in clean uniforms approached the paratroopers, relieved them, and took the positions.

"When we move, you and DeMarco's men take the lead," Wilson said

Kelly tightened his jaw. "You think Tony will make it?"

Wilson tapped him on the shoulder. "I'm holding the position in his platoon open for him." He headed to the rear area.

Kelly hobbled to Al.

Al, now a Staff Sergeant, raised his helmet above the bandage on his forehead. "Ya okay, lieutenant?"

"Yeah, a little stiff. There's hot chow behind the lines. After we eat, we're moving east. I'll be with your platoon. We'll take the point and lead the company."

"Are we that good, sir?"

Kelly shrugged.

Al walked to Rivers and Squeals, the platoon radio operator. "Let's go, we're movin out. There's hot chow ready for us a short ways back."

Rivers may have been tired, but he scrambled his feet. "What we havin to eat, sarge?"

"Steak. Your watta buffalo got shot. The cooks found him wit his legs pointin in the air. Someone in Alpha Company said Paw or Boom were bored with hunting Germans and took him out."

Squeals laughed. "Does a buffalo have a T-bone?"

Rivers waved his arm. "Y'all are both full of shit. We ain't eatin buffalo?"

Al slapped him on the back. "Stick wit me, kid. Sergeant DeMarco will be back soon, and he doesn't want ya hurt." He looked at the small bandage on Rivers' finger. "How's ya finger?"

Rivers raised his hand. "Don't know, still missing in action."

Chapter XII

THE GRENADE

Sweat dropped to the end of Mayer's nose. He bit into the gag across his mouth and shook the drop from his face. His hands, tied behind his back, pulled at the rope securing them and his legs to his desk chair. How could he have thought the girl and the dead Italian partisan were alone and others not nearby? He should have known Italian partisans, or the Americans, would send patrols into the mountains. After spending the last two hours thinking about what happened, he could not decide what made him so stupid. She was beautiful, her body was impressive, but she could not be over eighteen, young enough to be his granddaughter. *Why was she with them?*

Rather than dwell on his mistake, he kept his body stone still while he worked his hands to loosen the rope. Sweat poured down his face and into his narrowed eyes. He spotted morning sunshine entering the bottom edge of the tent. The loud squeal of air raid sirens made his heart jump. He looked at the canvas wall separating the two sections.

A private burst into the room. "Planes are..." He saw Schmitz's body and froze.

Mayer moaned and motioned with his head.

The soldier jumped in front of him. "Colonel, let me help you."

Mayer sucked in a deep breath from around the edges of the gag. His heart raced and a pain shot across his chest. Should the soldier overreact and try to pull him from the chair, they both would die. *Untie the gag,* he thought. Mayer shook his head and mumbled through the gag. "Nooo."

The young soldier snapped to attention.

Mayer grunted and bit down on the material in his mouth.

The young man leapt to his side and removed the gag.

"I am sitting on an American grenade, reach under me and get it. Be very careful."

The soldier, now teeming with fear, looked at Mayer's crotch and swallowed.

"Hurry. Make sure you hold the safety lever."

The soldier glanced from side to side, lowered his head, and stared at Mayer's thighs. He kneeled in front of his commander and slid a quivering hand between Mayer's legs. Their eyes made contact, and he grinned, pushing his hand further under Mayer's crotch. The young man's gaze shifted from side to side. When his fingers wiggled, Mayer's reaction was to tighten his muscles to protect his ass. He felt the grenade move as the private's fingers circled it and pulled it from under him.

"Sir, where is the safety pin?"

Mayer's face tightened and his teeth clamped together. "I didn't put the grenade there dumb ass... untie me."

The young man looked at the grenade and then around the room.

"Hurry!"

"Yes, Sir." He leaned over to set the grenade in front of Mayer's chair.

Mayer flinched and rocked back, a look of terror flashed across his face. "Don't put it on the floor! Hold it and untie me."

###

Mayer dashed from the tent and looked around the supply depot. Antiaircraft and machine guns fired into the sky. Soldiers scrambled in every direction to get away from fires burning near the stacked barrels of fuel. Those more dedicated, carried ammunition to men at the guns.

He looked into the sky. A plane, heading directly at the tent, released a bomb and pulled out of the dive.

Mayer's eyes focused on the bomb. It wiggled, turning its nose to earth, and settled into a smooth decent on a direct path toward him. He whipped around and scrambled inside his command center.

The tent exploded.

Chapter XIII

THE PLANE CRASH

The deafening sounds of bombers, fighters, bombs exploding and antiaircraft guns surrounded Tony and Anna.

"It was a mistake to stay around to watch," Tony said. He took Anna's hand. "Go first; you know the way out of here. I'll be right behind you."

She hesitated and swung her head from side to side.

Tony shook her. "Hurry, let's go."

Anna took off between trees and Tony kept pace with her.

The high pitch scream of a plane in a deep dive sent shivers through Tony's body. *Damn that's close!* He threw Anna to the ground the instant machine gun bullets cut across the path ten feet away. Tony shoved her against the base of a tree and covered her with his body. The plane's engine faded, and he jumped up, pulling her to her feet.

She pointed down the hillside. "Take that path down the mountain."

"I'll go first. Germans running from the explosions may be nearby. How long do we stay on this trail?" he asked.

"Until it leads to a clearing at the base of the mountain."

"Let me know when you need to rest," Tony said.

They raced downhill for the next hour before the land flattened.

Anna, panting and clutching her side, grabbed his arm. "There's a stream to the right. Let's stop and rest."

Tony took her hand. "How far?"

"Less than fifty meters."

"We'll walk slow, come."

They turned off the trail and approached the edge of a narrow mountain creek. Anna sat to catch her breath, and Tony kneeled beside her, filling his hand with water. He poured it over the back of her neck.

She bent her head forward and closed her eyes. "That feels good."

Tony wet both hands and rubbed her neck and forehead.

Anna took his hand and pressed it against her cheek.

He leaned over and kissed her forehead. "Get a good drink. I'll fill my canteen with cold water. We need to keep moving."

After a thirty-minute walk, they stopped.

Anna pointed along the trail. "Over there, the sun is bright... that's the field where Dario is waiting."

Tony nodded. "How far is it to your house?"

"Less than two hours once we meet him."

A plane's engine sputtered. The sound approached and grew louder. Tony scanned the treetops and saw smoke trailing from a fighter heading toward the clearing. *Five feet above the trees, might not make it.*

He and Anna ran to the edge of the clearing.

A furrow cut in the dirt led to the wreckage. The plane lay on its belly, the engine smoldering. Tony took off toward it.

Bullet holes snaked their way along the fuselage to the open cockpit. *Somehow, he got the canopy open.* He leapt onto the wing and grabbed the skirt of the cockpit.

The pilot's unbuckled harness hung loose on his shoulders. The young aviator's head rested against a shattered instrument panel. Blood covered his face and neck. Tony glanced at the bullet holes in the man's jacket.

Anna waited on the grass beside the wing. "Pull him out!"

Tony shook his head. "He's dead... didn't have a chance."

Tony's muscles stiffened when an artillery shell whizzed overhead. He leapt from the wing and shoved Anna to the ground. Dirt rained down on them from an explosion in front of the plane.

Anna held her hands over her ears and Tony pulled her to her feet. "Get away from the plane. The next one will be closer."

They dashed toward a thick line of trees across the field. An explosion knocked both of them off their feet.

Anna's pulse and heartbeat raced out of control but she heard nothing. *It's too quiet.* She opened her eyes, wiped dirt from her face and saw Tony lying on his back next to her. Her eyes widened, and she gasped. Blood soaked the fabric of the shirt on his left shoulder. The pack's strap lay in two pieces, as if cut with a sharp blade. She rolled to her knees, bent over and grabbed his shoulders. "Tony, get up!" Blood seeped between the fingers of her right hand and a pain shot across her chest. Lightheaded, she felt a wave of dizziness. "No. Please, no."

A hand grabbed her arm, but she ignored it. Nothing mattered any more. The one man who treated her like a woman, lay dying in the field, and she could do nothing.

"Get up," a male voice said.

She thrust an arm to the side waving him away.

Fingers of a firm hand tightened on her shoulder. "I said get up!"

Anna, concerned with keeping Tony alive, did not move. He had stood up for her with the American lieutenants and saved her from the Germans. She froze, watching his life ebbing away.

Two strong hands grabbed her under the arms and pulled her to the feet. "We need to go." The man turned her toward him.

She fought to focus on Dario's face.

"Run to the trees... I'll carry him." He shoved her, and she bolted toward the tree line.

Anna reached the donkey cart and leaned against a wheel to keep her balance. She wiped tears with her bloody hand, smearing red streaks across her cheeks. A strong acid taste filled her mouth. She wrapped her arms around her stomach, leaned over, heaved and sobbed.

Dario staggered to the back of the cart with Tony's limp body over his shoulder. He placed him into the back and dropped the weapon and pack beside him.

"Anna, get in," he said.

She stared at him, confused, by his simple command.

Dario removed a cloth from the cart and wiped blood and tears from her face. "Get in the cart. We need to take him to the house. Hold him and keep him as steady as possible."

Her surroundings, blurred by the trauma, began to sharpen. *I can't let him die.* She climbed into the back of the cart and helped him position Tony's head on her lap.

He leapt to the cart's seat and raised the lead to the donkey.

Chapter XIV

CARE AND COMFORT

Dario pulled on the rope around the donkey's neck and the cart stopped near the front door of the farmhouse. He jumped off and noticed blood covering Anna's hands and pants. "Are you hurt?"

"No." She raised her hands and wiped them on her shirt. "It's his blood, help me."

He helped slide Tony from her lap. "Go inside, I'll carry him and come back for the guns."

###

Anna bolted into the house and ran to her bedroom. She wiped her hands on a towel and threw it into a corner. Turning to the bed, she yanked the bedspread off the double mattress and let it to fall to the floor. The standing mirror in the middle of the room wobbled when she bumped into it. She slid it beside a tall dresser. Tony would stay in her room. She knew she could use the couch until he recovered.

Dario carried Tony into the room and lowered him onto the mattress.

Anna went to the kitchen, filled a pot with water and carried it back to the room. She ripped a clean sheet into strips.

She glanced at Tony, saw he was half undressed, and turned to Dario.

"I put his shirt, boots and the dagger in the corner," he said.

"Thank you." Her hands shook as she stared at the wound. "It looks bad. The hole's big, but the bleeding stopped."

"He said something while you were out of the room."

"Were you going to tell me?" she asked.

"It made little sense."

"What was it?"

He shrugged his shoulders. "Get the red house."

"He lost a lot of blood. I need to clean the wound and cover it." She picked up two pieces of cloth. "Go heat a large pot of water. When you light the fire, keep adding paper and wet wood. Someone will see the smoke and contact Uncle Luca."

Dario left the room.

Anna cleaned Tony's wound with wet pieces of linen and stepped to the dresser. From the bottom drawer, she removed a large bottle of clear liquid. She pulled the cork, dribbled liquid on a clean piece of cloth, and placed it over Tony's wound.

That night, Anna woke when she felt something touch her arm and heard Dario's voice.

"Tony opened his eyes."

She jumped off the couch and raced to her bedroom. Leaning over the bed, she kissed him. "Thank God you're awake."

His gaze drifted around the room, his voice barely audible. "Where am I?"

"My house, metal from the explosion is in your shoulder."

"It's numb."

"You need a doctor."

Tony glanced at the door. "Where's Luca?"

"He'll be here soon."

Each time Tony's eyes closed, they remained shut longer.

"Get the red..." he mumbled.

Anna did not hear the rest of his words. She leaned to him. "What?"

"Get the red signal panel from my pack."

"What do you want me to do with it?"

His eyes blinked and lips moved but made no intelligible sound.

"Don't shut your eyes, keep talking."

She watched his eyelids flutter and fight to stay open.

"Put it on the house," he mumbled.

Dario rushed into the room.

"Why?" Anna asked Tony.

"It's a..." His eyes closed.

"What did he say?" Dario asked.

"Get the red panel that's in his backpack."

Dario cocked his head to the side. "That's what he said earlier."

"Put it on the house," Anna said.

"Do you want it on the roof?"

Anna jerked both hands up in front of her. "I don't know... near the front door!"

Luca stood outside the front door and glanced at the pink predawn horizon. He removed his MP-40 from his shoulder, brushed dirt from his clothes and pushed open the door. He saw Dario's hand, slide to a submachine gun leaning against the couch. "It's me, Dario."

Dario swung his feet to the floor and stood.

"You don't look good. How's Anna?"

"She's fine. Tony is hurt."

"Where is he?"

"In her bedroom."

Luca headed to Anna's room, Dario followed. She lay asleep on a bedspread on the floor. He glanced at Tony and motioned Dario out of the room.

They entered the living room and passed through rays of morning sunlight coming in the window.

"His radio should be in his pack. Get it," Luca ordered.

Dario carried Tony's backpack to the large table and removed a shattered radio. Luca picked it up, inspected the damage, and shoved it back into the pack. Dario followed him out the front door and both leaned their weapons against the side of the house.

Luca looked at the red panel nailed to the wall beside the door. "What's that red cloth?"

Dario shrugged. "Tony told Anna to put it there."

Luca pulled a crumbled pack of Lucky Strike cigarettes from his pocket and lit one. "Thank God she wasn't hurt."

"Were you with the Americans?" Dario asked.

"Yes. We listened to the pilots on the radio."

"What happened?"

Luca smiled. "I think the Germans will leave now."

The door opened. Anna ran into Luca's arms and kissed his cheeks. "How long have you been here?"

"Less than an hour. How's Tony?"

"Not good." She leaned her head to his shoulder and wrapped her arms around him.

Luca held her. "You reached for his heart and gave him yours. Don't decide until you're sure."

"You don't understand," she said.

"I do."

Anna pulled away from him and shook her head. "No, you don't."

"Anna, you're still a girl."

Anna glared at him and shook her head. Tears formed. "The Germans captured me! Tony saved my life."

Luca glanced at the ground. He snapped back toward her. "Where's Gino?"

Two hours later, Tony, wearing civilian clothes, lay in bed supported by pillows. Anna sat on the edge of the bed and cradled his hand.

"How long did I sleep?"

"Over fifteen hours."

He looked at the bandage and his clothes. "Who did this?"

Anna smiled and raised her eyebrows.

Tony pushed against the mattress, straining to raise himself with his uninjured arm.

She placed a hand on his shoulder. "Don't, you'll bleed again."

"It burns like hell, what did you put on it?"

Anna reached to the floor beside the bed and picked up the corked bottle. She held it in front of him. "Grappa... to kill the infection."

Luca strolled into the room and glanced at the bottle in Anna's hand. He smiled. "You are drinking?"

Tony grinned and shook his head. "No, I'm bathing in it."

Luca scrunched his eyebrows and furrowed his brow.

Anna shrugged. "Alcohol for the wound."

Tony patted Anna's leg. "Sounds good."

Luca walked to the bed. "The Americans need to know you're here. I'll contact Major Franklin."

"What happened in the mountains?" Tony asked.

"The pilots that returned talked about shooting a bird."

"What do you mean? Anna asked."

"They called it a turkey shoot."

"I know what they meant," Tony said. "When you speak to Major Franklin, tell him to get the lieutenants out of the mountains."

"What does 'turkey shoot' mean?" Anna asked.

Tony grinned. "Shooting at slow, easy to hit targets."

Luca nodded. "Rest, Anna will take care of you."

Chapter XV

THE NAZI FLAG

Al walked ahead of Kelly and the remaining members of the platoon. He watched the point man, ten yards in front of him, glanced around and smiled. Every man moved through the trees with deliberate and alert caution.

A rumor spread among the men that Italian partisans, along with a few American soldiers, coordinated air strikes against German supply lines. The losses suffered by the Germans made it possible for the paratroopers to press the attack northward. Al's gut feeling was that Sergeant DeMarco had his hand in whatever happened. *It can't be easy out there. Maybe now he'll come back.*

The Point Man flashed an exaggerated arm signal, ran back and dove to the ground. Al motioned his men down, dropped to the ground, and readied his Thompson. He heard German voices. *They're loud as hell. Not worried about getting into a fight.*

Six German soldiers, bunched together, came into view. Al focused on the man in front carrying an MP-40 submachine gun on a sling around his neck. That weapon pinned him as the leader of the patrol and his path led toward Al.

The patrol leader stopped, extended an arm to his side, and scanned the terrain in front of him. He pointed in Al's direction.

Al's chest tightened and his breathing quickened. *If he didn't see me, he's blind.* His finger pulled back the trigger and the Thompson opened up on full automatic. Paratroopers around him fired.

The German patrol leader's weapon fired on full automatic and bullets ripped into the ground around the paratroopers. Al watched bullets slam into the man's chest, the muzzle of his MP-40 lifted and cut leaves from the trees. The paratroopers continued to fire until the six Germans fell. Al and his men jumped up and moved forward to check for signs of life.

"Anyone hit?" Kelly yelled.

"No, sir," Al replied.

"Check for documents and bust up the weapons," Kelly said.

Al turned toward his men. "Rivers, get the guns." He waited for a response.

Someone yelled, "medic!"

Al turned toward the voice and saw paratroopers standing over a body. He ran to them and arrived the same time as Doc.

They dropped beside the body and stared at a bullet hole in the man's helmet.

"Jesus, that's Rivers," Doc said.

Al slumped beside the body. "No." His mouth went dry, and a lump formed in his throat. "His eighteenth birthday is next week."

When Doc reached out to lift the helmet, it moved. He snatched it from Rivers' head.

Rivers rolled to his back and squinted at Al. He struggled to a sitting position and shook his head. "What ya lookin at?" he asked Al.

"Let me check you out," Doc said. He rubbed his hand across the side Rivers' head.

"Ouch."

Doc stood. "It's just a bruise... must have knocked him out." He plodded away.

"You're lucky kid. Don't get shot again because Sergeant DeMarco will kill me," Al said. He handed Rivers his helmet. "Ya betta get a new one."

"This one works," Rivers said, rubbing the bullet hole. "Wait till Sergeant DeMarco sees it."

Luca stood in the front yard smoking a cigarette. Dario walked out the door with his submachine gun slung across his chest. Luca looked at his weapon leaning against the side of the house and back at Dario. *He hated the old rifle. Now he has that thing and goes nowhere without it.*

"I'm worried about Anna," Dario said.

Dario would do anything to protect his cousin, and he would not let the subject of Anna and Tony rest. Luca helped insure both his niece and nephew grew-up making their own decisions, but Dario always thought her judgment needed further review. Interceding in the choices adults make, was something he did not want to do. He looked at his nephew and shook his head. "I know."

"She's falling in love with Tony."

"I know, Dario."

"When he leaves here, he won't return."

Luca raised his eyes. "I'll speak to her later."

"Tony's life is in America, he doesn't want to live here," Dario said.

Luca held his hands behind his back and tightened his jaw "I don't know what Tony wants and neither do you. Half his family is in America and half in Italy. For now, he must follow orders and fight this war."

"She should forget him. Everything she needs is here."

Luca, exhaled, raised both his hands in front of his nephew. "Dario, your cousin will decide what she wants and needs. Her heart may be a big part of her decision. I suggest you quit worrying about her."

"It's a mistake."

"She's a woman, one year younger than you. Learn to respect her decisions."

"She's a girl, Uncle Luca."

Luca's head ached and his chest tightened. He reminded himself to stay calm. "Say that to her one more time, Dario, and she will knock you on your ass. Let's hope the Americans are moving this way, Tony needs help."

The paratroopers of Bravo Company reached the crest of the hill and set up a perimeter. Al and Rivers dropped to the ground under a tree. Rivers kept his eyes on Wilson and

Kelly, talking at the top of the hill. *Wonder what they're talking about?* "I'll be right back." He strolled to a spot near the officers. Without attracting attention, he sat beside a tree, and listened.

Wilson raised a set of binoculars, spent a moment surveying the landscape below the hill, and handed them to Kelly. "Tell me what you think."

Kelly looked through the field glasses for a minute and turned back to Wilson. "Two men and two Schmeissers."

"You think they're Germans?"

Kelly shrugged and looked a second time. "The tall one has blond hair, doesn't look Italian. That red cloth hanging near the door may be part of a Nazi flag."

"Is that it?" Wilson asked.

"I think so."

"Did you see a swastika?"

Kelly adjusted the focus. "No, just a piece of red canvas."

Wilson nodded. "Okay, tell me about the house."

"It's stone... solid. Might be loaded with Germans, but the two in the yard are the only ones I see."

"That's what worries me." Wilson knelt and removed a map from his pocket. "You got any suggestions?"

Kelly pulled the binoculars from his eyes and stared at the ground. "We could send a platoon."

Wilson frowned and shook his head. "Better think twice... might not be a good idea. There's a lot of open area between the trees and the house. Easy targets... if someone unloaded with a machine gun, they'd get slaughtered."

Kelly grinned at his commander. "I'll bet a week's pay I can drop the first round of artillery next to the red panel."

"Then what?" Wilson asked.

"If anyone runs out the door, I'll take the house down to ground level."

Wilson's gaze bounced between the map and Kelly. He turned to the radio operator. "Give Lieutenant Kelly the handset so he can call in artillery."

Rivers jumped up and ran to Al, sitting, with his eyes shut, against a tree. "Al, ya gotta watch this."

"Watch what?"

Rivers pointed at the two officers. "The lieutenant."

"No thanks. Every time he looks at me and says something, a German takes a shot at my ass."

"No, he's bettin the captain a whole weeks pay."

Al shrugged. "It's his money."

"Lieutenant Kelly's gonna call in artillery on a farmhouse."

"What farmhouse?"

"The one with a red Nazi flag on it."

Al's eyes sprang open, and he leaned away from the tree. "There's a Nazi flag on a farmhouse?"

"Well, not a Nazi flag... no swastika, just a red panel."

The blood drained from Al's face. He scrambled to his feet and took off toward the officers. *He's runnin like a man being chased by a bayou alligator.* Rivers grabbed Al's submachine gun and raced after him.

"No lieutenant, stop!" Al yelled.

Wilson and Kelly spun toward him. Kelly removed the radio handset from his ear. Wilson planted his feet and locked his eyes on Al. "Are you nuts, sergeant?"

He froze. "No, sir, it's Sergeant DeMarco."

"Where?"

"The red panel, sir."

Rivers and the nearby group of men moved close to the conversation.

The soldier next to him whispered. "Sergeants didn't run up to the company officers and shout at them."

This was a first for Rivers and he didn't want to miss the next few minutes.

Wilson tilted his head to the side and furrowed his brow. "This better be good, Sergeant Bertone."

"Sir, Sergeant DeMarco has been carryin part of a red drop zone panel since we left North Africa."

"When did you have this dream?"

"He showed it to me before he left Sicily."

"You come running up here screaming about a red DZ marker and you've seen nothing yet? You think that's what is on the house down there?"

Al sucked in a breath of air. "Yes, sir. Rivers said it was."

The company commander looked around and spotted him.

Rivers nodded. It was the first time Captain Wilson locked eyes with him and his expression was not a smile. "That's what the lieutenant said, sir."

Wilson handed Al the binoculars, and he looked at the farmhouse. "That's it, sir, I'm sure. Ya gotta go there."

Every paratrooper watching the officers froze. Staff sergeants did not make decisions for officers.

Wilson glared at him. "Me? I have to go? Who died and made you the company commander?"

"I'll go, sir. I know that's..."

Wilson cut him off and shoved his index finger at him. "You bet you will. I'm not getting a bunch of men killed because of a wild hair across your ass."

The group of paratroopers pressed together, their focus bouncing from Sergeant Bertone to Captain Wilson. Al might have put himself in danger, but after the commander's comment, no one would say a word. Rivers glanced at them. *They don't want their big mouths getting ahead of their hummingbird asses.*

"What happens if he's wrong?" Kelly asked.

Wilson did not look at Al as he spoke to Kelly. "You call in artillery... the house disappears in a massive explosion. Staff Sergeant Bertone's ass becomes little pieces of flesh and bone." He looked at Al and raised his shoulders. "Still think you're right, Sergeant Bertone?"

"Yes, sir," Al said.

A slow smile built on Wilson's face. "Then move out, and good luck."

Al passed through the crowd of silent paratroopers.

Rivers handed him his Thompson submachine gun. "Be careful," he whispered.

Luca and Dario stood in the front yard talking. Luca saw movement inside the tree line. "Someone's coming."

Dario slid his hands to his weapon.

"Wait, Dario."

They watched a soldier with a Thompson hanging across his chest emerge from the trees. The man held his arms at his side with his palms facing forward as he marched toward the house.

"What's he doing?" Dario asked. He raised his weapon and swung the barrel toward the soldier.

Luca swept a hand to the top of Dario's gun and pushed the muzzle toward the ground. "He hasn't threatened us and there's got to be more of them in the trees."

The soldier continued his slow march.

Luca grabbed Dario's arm and waved with his free hand. "Look at the baggy pants he's wearing. He's an American paratrooper."

The soldier increased his pace.

"Hurry," Luca yelled.

Dario waved the man towards them.

The paratrooper broke into a run.

Without speaking, the men shook hands and slapped each other on the back.

"There's an American sergeant here with us," Luca said.

"Sergeant DeMarco. Is he hurt?" the soldier asked.

Luca's mouth fell open, and he stared at the soldier. "How did you know?"

Al pointed at the canvas nailed to the wall. "Because of that. I'm Al Bertone."

"I'm Luca Amati, this is my nephew Dario."

The front door flew open and Anna stepped into the doorway. Her wet dark hair fell across the thin straps of her clean cotton dress.

Al filled his lungs, expanding his chest. His lips pressed together.

Anna looked him over and turned to Dario. "Who is this?" She stepped in front of Al before Dario could answer. "What's your name?"

Al's warrior stance withered. "Bertone... Uh, Al, Miss. Sergeant Alphonse Bertone."

"You're American and Italian?" she asked.

"Yes, ma'am, Sicilian."

"Why are you here?"

"To help Sergeant DeMarco."

Anna's eyes widened. She grabbed his arm. "Come in, quick."

Al raised his arm waving the OK sign toward the paratroopers on the hill.

She pulled him into the house.

Luca and Dario turned to the trees and saw more paratroopers headed toward the house.

Chapter XVI

THE HOSPITAL

Tony heard whispering beside the bed. Someone said, "Tell the guys to get a medic," but he didn't recognize the voice until he heard, "Sarge, it's Al."

He focused on the blurry figure. "How'd you find me?" The smile on Al's face came into focus.

"Dance of the red panel. Ya didn't wave it so I figured you were hurt."

"Wave it? I can't even scratch the left cheek of my ass."

Al looked at the bandaged shoulder. "How ya feelin?"

"Like somebody burned a hole in me."

"We'll get ya outta here."

Kelly ran into the room. "Damn, can he walk?"

"I'm not dead yet, Lieutenant."

Al and Kelly helped Tony from the bed. They walked to the couch in the living room and lowered Tony onto it.

Al looked down at him. "Ya look like hell."

Tony pointed at the stripes on Bertone's sleeve. "Whose staff sergeant stripes did you steal?"

Al tapped his upper arm. "Whatever ya said to the captain worked."

Tony tightened his jaw, his stomach churned. He could not be sure he would get the answer he wanted, but he had to ask. "How's the kid?"

Al grinned, nodding his head. "He's okay... cut a finger."

Anna walked into the room wiping tears from her cheeks. Tony took her hand when she reached the couch and pulled her down beside him.

"Where are you taking him?" she asked Kelly.

"To a hospital in Salerno."

"Can he take his backpack and clothes?"

"Sure," Kelly said. He tapped Al's arm and tilted his head toward the door. They walked out of the house.

Anna squeezed Tony's arm. "Can I go with you?"

"You're safer here."

"Will I see you again?"

He stroked her face. "Yes, but I don't know when." He pulled her to him.

###

Anna stood near Luca, a few feet from the front door. A civilian backpack hung from one of her shoulders. Soldiers dug holes in the yard and stacked whatever material they found to make defensive positions.

She watched a jeep drive up the cart path and stop in front of Luca. A soldier, with a red cross on his helmet, leapt from the back seat and ran into the house. Anna watched an officer step from the jeep. She recognized the captain's insignia on the front of his helmet.

He walked to Luca. "I saw you in Sicily, didn't I?" Wilson said.

Luca nodded. "Yes, at Major Franklin's office. I'm Luca Amati."

Wilson extended his hand. "I'm Paul Wilson, Sergeant DeMarco's commander. Are you the one who helped him?"

"My niece and nephew did."

"I want to talk to them, later."

The soldier with the red cross on his helmet helped Tony out the front door.

"How you doing?" Wilson asked.

"A little sore, sir."

"I'll keep the slot open for you."

"I'll take it, sir. Give me a week to recover."

"Report back when the doctors finish," Wilson said. He turned to Anna.

"You're Luca's niece?"

"Yes."

"Can I talk to you a moment?"

"Can I help Tony first?" she said.

Wilson nodded.

She and the medic helped Tony into the jeep and the soldier walked away. She dropped the pack onto the backseat floorboard.

Anna leaned her head against Tony's arm. Staring at the floorboard of the jeep, time slowed. "I'll wait for you. Please come back."

"I promise I will." The jeep engine started as he pulled Anna to him and kissed her.

Anna watched the jeep disappear into the trees. She wiped her eyes and did not see Wilson behind her.

"I'm Captain Wilson."

"I'm Anna."

"Your uncle said you helped Sergeant DeMarco."

"Yes."

"Can you tell me what happened?"

"Yes, let's go inside."

After a month in the hospital, Tony was well on his way to recovery. He sat on the edge of his bed, exercised his left arm and glanced around the hospital ward. Twenty beds with wounded soldiers filled the room. Nurses on duty stood by those in serious condition while medics trudged from bed to bed.

The room looked nothing like the day he arrived. Plaster filled the old bullet holes and a fresh coat of whitewash covered the walls and ceiling. Somewhere out of thin air, white sheets appeared on each bed. The day he woke after surgery, a nurse told him the Navy demanded improvements be made, and provided the material and personnel to complete the job. *Sailors don't like sleeping in dirt.*

He glanced at the photo of old man in a fedora leaning against a glass on the table beside the bed.

Senior medic, Staff Sergeant Jerry Zeller, walked up behind him and set a backpack on the bed. "This was in the storage room."

"Damn, I forgot I brought it."

"It was at the bottom of the pile. Sorry I didn't find it sooner."

Tony opened the backpack. A photo of Anna lay on top of clean civilian clothes and the bottle of Grappa. He pushed the clothes to the side and saw his dagger and Anna's Luger. Tony removed the photo and closed the pack.

Jerry leaned in and looked at the picture. "Wow, she's beautiful... that your wife?"

"No, a girl I met. She's the reason I'm alive."

"She looks Italian."

"Yeah, she lives southeast of here."

Jerry raised his eyebrows. "A local girl."

Major Towers, the surgeon who operated on Tony, entered the ward. He held a folded uniform, pair of brown jump boots and an overseas hat with a glider patch. "Afternoon, Tony. How's the shoulder?"

"Great Doc, when do the stitches come out?"

"Maybe a week." He dropped the uniform and boots into a chair. "Your unit sent these when they passed through here. They've made quite a name for themselves. The first into Naples and now they are kicking ass to the north."

"Can I join them?" Tony asked.

"Not yet, but we could use this bed."

"Where do I go?"

Towers grinned. "Two weeks convalescent leave in Salerno."

"What about a place to stay?"

"Jerry will set you up at a hotel."

Tony picked up the uniform and looked at the stripes on the sleeve. "I'm not a Sergeant First Class."

Towers slapped him on the back. "You are now. Promotion orders are in the pocket, congratulations."

"Thank you, sir."

"Get with Jerry at least twice. He'll take the stitches out and make sure the wound is healing."

Tony extended his hand. "Thank you for all you've done, Major."

Towers shook his hand. "No problem. Take care of yourself." He walked to another patient.

"Get dressed and we'll meet when you're done getting paid. Don't forget your dad's photo," Jerry said.

Tony and Jerry stood outside of a building with 'Finance' scribbled above the door. Tony stuffed a wad of cash into his pocket.

"What's the situation with the Germans?" he asked Jerry.

"After your guys liberated Naples, the Germans withdrew north. Everything from there south is in our hands."

"Good. I need a big favor."

Jerry raised his eyebrows and grinned. "Does this have something to do with the young and beautiful local girl?"

Tony nodded.

"What can I do to help?"

"If anyone asks, I came to see you. I have two weeks to do something important. I'll take care of the stitches."

Jerry handed him a piece paper. "This is the directions to the hotel... in case you need it."

Tony removed the bottle of Grappa from his backpack. "This is for you... homemade Grappa. Sip it... burns like hell."

They shook hands and Tony headed into downtown Salerno. He dodged military traffic and said hello to Italian shopkeepers standing in the doorways. He adjusted the civilian pack slung over his good shoulder and stopped to look at Jerry's directions.

Tony turned onto a main street and glanced at Italian workers repairing damage to buildings along the street. The name of the hotel he was looking for protruded above a door thirty feet in front of him. He stopped in the doorway and looked up the street. Two army jeeps sat in front of a bar sign hanging above open double doors. He stepped into the hotel entrance.

After midnight, Tony, attired in civilian clothes, emerged from the hotel. He strolled toward the bar. The jeeps had not moved, and he stopped outside the bar entrance to listen to music and the loud voices of drunks and barmaids. Stepping between the jeeps, he tapped two gas cans on the back of the first jeep. *The sound of full gas cans.*

Tony crossed the street, leaned against a building and kept his eyes on the bar door.

An overweight sergeant wearing a sullied uniform tramped from the bar and plopped into the passenger seat of the first jeep. *Tubby,* Tony thought. An inebriated sergeant, held up by a giddy young barmaid, staggered into the doorway.

The drunk slurred his words. "Can't leave now."

"You're drunk," Tubby said.

"Yup. I know."

"No more drinks. When you sober up, we leave."

The drunk leaned over the barmaid and kissed her. "Sounds good to us."

The sergeants returned to the bar.

Tony gave the jeeps a once over and looked up and down the street. *Transportation problem solved.* He strolled to the front jeep, dropped his backpack onto the passenger seat and jumped behind the wheel. *A pissed off officer will be walking.* He started the engine and drove away.

Chapter XVII

THE GRAVES

The morning sun broke over the mountains while Tony drove south on the main road leading out of Salerno. No need to rush, the military police would look for the jeep in the city and the sergeants would not want to talk about their stupidity. He pulled off the deserted road and changed into his uniform. Now he looked like an American soldier driving an American jeep.

Ten minutes down the road, a sawhorse blockade barred the path. Two soldiers, military policemen, stood behind it.

A tall sergeant, with three stripes on his sleeves, and the upside down arrow patch of the 36TH Infantry Division near his shoulder, stood in the center of the road with both hands on his hips. Beside him, a short, skinny private held on to a wooden pole blocking the road, as if it could stop a speeding vehicle.

Tony hit the brakes and skidded to a standstill inches from the blockade. A checkpoint on the road out of Salerno was not part of his plan. He placed his left leg on the ground and stood. "Move that thing."

"Need to see your travel orders," the sergeant said.

Tony looked to the jeep's floorboard. The silenced Luger lay inside the open backpack. He leaned over, grabbed the pack and raised it into the air. "I'm a courier for General Clark's headquarters."

The sergeant must have noticed the stripes on Tony's uniform. He took his hands from his hips and straightened his back. "You got written orders, sarge?"

Tony glared at him. "Who you with?"

"The 36th."

Give a buck sergeant a little authority and he becomes Caesar. "My men already saved your asses once." Tony held the pack in the air. "If these plans don't get through, your guys are gonna get the shit kicked out of them like they did on the beach south of here." He tossed the backpack on the passenger's seat. "Think they had time stop the war and type orders?"

The private glanced back and forth between Tony and the sergeant. "Better let him pass, Frank."

"He needs to have written orders," Frank said.

"Fine. I'll go back and get'em." Tony dropped into the seat. *What do I do now?* He grabbed the windshield, sprang up and pointed at the sergeant. "When I get back to Salerno, the colonel at headquarters will ask a lot of questions. I want to tell him who sent me back... he might have a few questions for you. What's your last name, Frank?"

"Martin."

"And you?" Tony asked the private.

"Saul, sarge."

Tony sighed and shook his head. *A replacement that arrived last week.* "Did your mother name you after me, or you got a last name of your own?"

Saul stiffened and his mouth fell open. "Gold... Goldberg, sir. Saul Goldberg."

"Don't sir me!" Tony slapped the stripes on his uniform sleeve. "See these fucking Sergeant First Class stripes?"

"Yes, sir... sarge."

"I'm not an officer, I work for a living."

Martin's mouth hung open and his gaze ping-ponged between Tony, and the pole blocking the road. He shuffled his feet, lifted the pole and pushed it from the road.

The jeep lurched forward and stopped beside the two men. "Goldberg," Tony said.

"Sir."

Tony raised his head and eyes. *The kid deserves a little sympathy.* "If the Germans come anywhere near here, run and hide." He popped the clutch and sped away.

The jeep raced up the cart path in front of Anna's house and Tony spotted someone near the large tree. He slammed on the brakes, raising a cloud of dust in the front yard. Tony lifted the backpack. Without hesitating, he raced around the corner of the house and looked at the flowers at the base of the tree. He grinned when he saw the girl kneeling before two wooden crosses amongst a bed of white flowers.

The closer he came to the girl, the faster his heart pounded in his chest and his feet moved. He took off running and stopped beside her.

"Anna!"

The girl he thought was Anna turned to him and tilted her head. "I'm Bianca."

Tony smiled at Anna's sister and glanced at the crosses. Both legs weakened and dizziness forced him to his knees. All he saw were the names Paolo and Anna on the freshly painted crosses. His mouth became dry and his hand shook when he ran his fingertips across the name Anna. "No... please," he said lowering his head.

Bianca touched his shoulder. "Tony?"

"Yes." His lips quivered. "When did it happen?"

"Seven years ago."

Tony blinked and repeated her words in his head. "What?"

Bianca studied him for a moment. "It was influenza and happened quite suddenly. When the Fascists killed my father we buried him beside her."

Tony's mouth hung open, and he stared at her "I don't understand. It couldn't have been seven years ago. I was with her last month."

"Not my sister... that's my mother's grave."

It took a moment for her words to register in his brain. He jumped to his feet. "Your mother's grave?"

"Yes."

"The crosses weren't here when I came."

"No, Uncle Luca brought them back two weeks ago. He repainted them."

Tony pointed at Anna's cross. "Anna was your mother? Where is your sister?"

"She's here."

The weakness in his legs disappeared. He let out a huge breath, wrapped his arms around Bianca and kissed her on both cheeks. He could not take his eyes off the beautiful Anna lookalike. "Anna was right."

Bianca cocked her head. "About what?"

"She told me you looked like twins."

Bianca laughed and pointed to a small stone outbuilding. "Anna's over there."

Tony turned and saw Anna coming out the door.

As she looked toward the tree, she stopped. Her hand covered her mouth and she raced toward him. "Tony!" She leapt into his arms and sobbed. Tears streamed down her cheeks as she kissed him. "I love you."

Tony flinched and turned the injured left shoulder away from her.

"Did I hurt you?"

"No, it's fine." He placed both hands on her upper arms and held her at arm's length, taking in her beauty.

"He thought it was your grave," Bianca said motioning toward the cross.

"Sorry, I never told you; I'm named after my mother."

"My heart stopped... I didn't know what to do," he said shaking his head. A grin turned to a large smile as he studied the two women. Without the different colored dresses and the different hairstyles, he couldn't tell them apart. "I'd swear you're twins."

Bianca sat in a chair in front of Tony and Anna, curled up next to him, on the couch. Each held a glass of wine.

"When did you come home?" he asked Bianca.

"Uncle Luca came to get me three weeks ago."

"Where is he?"

"In Salerno, helping the Americans," Anna said.

"I'm glad you came back," Bianca said.

He winked at her. "Maybe now your sister will trust me."

Bianca straightened her back and glanced at her sister. "For almost one month she hasn't eaten well; she's getting skinny. She stayed in the house, talked about you, and cried."

"Bianca!" Anna said.

Tony chuckled at the mischievous look on Bianca's face. *Sister's rivalry. She's a tease.*

"Every day she spent hours talking about how much she missed you. She told me everything about Ponte, your brothers and sisters and the night at the Roman tomb."

Anna squirmed. "Please, Bianca, enough. You are embarrassing me."

Tony strove to create his best quizzical expression. "Does she like me?"

Bianca jumped in her seat. "She loves you!"

A red flush crept across Anna's face. "Stop, both of you."

Tony and Bianca laughed. He pulled Anna to him and kissed her.

Bianca stood, raised her glass and finished her wine. "I have to help Dario and Uncle Luca tonight."

Anna held out her hand and her sister helped her to her feet. They embraced.

Tony shoved himself from the couch and kissed Bianca's cheek. "Tell Luca I said hello."

"I will. The three of us will come here in the morning." She waved and walked out the door.

Anna squeezed Tony's arm and rested her head against his shoulder. "I can't believe you're here."

"I made a promise, didn't I?"

"Yes."

"Tomorrow I'm going to Ponte. Will you come with me?"

Anna tipped her head. "Yes!" She paused. "What about Bianca, Dario and Uncle Luca?"

"We'll wait for them to arrive in the morning."

Tony, without his shirt, sat next to his backpack on the couch. Gauze and tape protruded from the open pack. He checked the new bandage on his shoulder and secured the last piece of tape. An empty glass stood next to a bottle of wine on the floor in front of the couch. Lifting the bottle, he filled the glass and took a drink. He leaned against the couch and shut his eyes.

The sound of footsteps brought him back to reality. He opened his eyes and saw Anna. Her wet hair lay across a simple button up dress. He reached out and took her hands. "I've never seen a girl as beautiful as you."

Anna leaned over, they kissed and she sat next to him. "How's your shoulder?"

Tony shrugged. "Have you ever removed stitches?"

"Many times, on a dress."

He nodded and smiled. "That should be good enough."

Anna pressed herself against him. "What will you do when the war ends?"

"I need to help my family and bring my father here to see his brothers and sisters."

"Will he come back to live in Italy?"

"No, but he wants to visit."

Anna squirmed and pressed against him.

Letters he received from his father and older sister told him they worried about his safety and the welfare of the family members in Ponte. His father said he wanted to visit Italy once the war ended. Overwhelmed by his family responsibilities, he had underestimated his desire to be with the woman next to him. He took her hand, raised it to his lips and kissed it. "When the war ends, the first thing I will do is come to this house. Then I will make arrangements for my father to come here, meet you and visit Ponte."

"Do you promise?"

Tony looked into her eyes, took her cheeks in his hands and tilted his head. "What can I do to make you believe me?"

"Kiss me."

He pulled her against his chest and wrapped his arms around her. Their first passionate kiss lingered.

"Will you wait?" Tony asked.

"Forever," she whispered.

Tony helped her stand, and they walked to her bedroom. Anna lay on the bed and he sat beside her. He ran his hands through her hair, stroked her face and kissed her neck.

"I love you," he whispered.

She pulled him to her and rubbed her body against his. "Please, Tony."

Chapter XVIII

PONTE

Tony, in his uniform, stepped out the front door. In one hand, he held the MP-40, in the other, his civilian pack. He marched to the jeep and placed the weapon and pack on the driver's seat. Leaning down he adjusted the pant legs bloused in his brown paratrooper boots.

Anna came out of the house wearing a white blouse, a long light blue skirt and sandals. She had pulled her dark long hair over one shoulder. He could not take his eyes off her. *I'm the luckiest man in earth.* She carried a large canvas shoulder bag and handed it to him.

"More food?" he asked.

"Not much this time, wine, bread and sausage."

He placed the bag on the back seat and took her into his arms. Pulling her against his body, he kissed her.

Luca, Bianca and Dario hurried around the corner of the house. Both men held their submachine guns to their chests.

Luca walked to Tony and hugged him. "You look good. I wanted to visit you in the hospital but Major Franklin was worried about me spending too much time on the streets of Salerno. There are still German spies in the city."

"I understand."

"Good morning," Dario said on his way to embrace Anna. He kissed her cheeks and turned to Tony. "I didn't think you would come back."

"You don't know me well."

Dario nodded and smiled.

"We're going to Ponte. Come with us... we can all go," Anna said.

"You sure it's safe?" Dario asked.

"I wouldn't go if it wasn't," said Tony. "Everything south of Naples is liberated."

Anna took her time as she moved to Dario's side.

"Uncle Luca and I have to go to Salerno," Bianca said. "I think you should go, Dario, we'll be fine."

Anna poked Dario in the side. "Okay?"

"Yes, I'll go."

"Where are your men now?" Luca asked.

"They're north of Naples."

"When do you need to return to them?"

"In two weeks. I have something important I want to discuss with you."

Luca nodded. "When you get back we will sit down and enjoy a glass of Anna's wine."

Everyone hugged and kissed. Tony and Anna took the front seats of the jeep. Dario jumped in the back.

Tony handed Dario his pack and weapon. "Put the bags over the guns. We need to cover the German weapons."

Tony drove the meandering mountain road into the Picentini Mountains. Along the route, he kept glancing at the distant city of Salerno. He imagined how much it had changed since the first day of the invasion. Allied ships now lined the few remaining docks while others, anchored in the harbor, unloaded their cargo onto small vessels. North of the port, the towns of the Amalfi coast dotted the near vertical hillside.

Tony slowed, navigated a narrow curve and approached a roadside fountain. Behind the fountain, a curved stone wall guarded a hillside and a town.

He turned the jeep from the road and stopped near the fountain.

An old man, in a black fedora, cocked to one side of his head, sat on the rock wall. He tapped a walking stick against the sole of his boot and watched them get out of the jeep.

Homes and the buildings covered the landscape on the other side of the wall. Anna pointed at them. "That may be Ponte."

Tony glanced at the old man who nodded and touched the brim of his fedora.

A local, Tony thought. He walked to him. "Excuse me. Do you live near here?"

The man turned and pointed over the wall. "Yes, in that town."

"Is that Ponte?"

"Yes."

"Good. I am looking for the house of the DeMarco family."

The old man pushed himself from the wall and rubbed the stubble on his cheek. "Why?"

Anna and Dario stepped to Tony and stood at his side.

"They are my family. Do you know which house they live in?"

The old man pressed his lips together and nodded. He tilted his fedora to the back of his head and studied Tony's uniform. "American?"

"Yes."

"What is your name?" he asked.

"Antonio... Antonio DeMarco."

The man removed his fedora and swept it toward the structures dotting the hillside past the wall. "See those houses?"

"Yes."

"A DeMarco lives in every house."

Tony's mouth dropped opened and his stomach fluttered.

The man took Tony's hand. "I am Durante DeMarco, your father's brother."

Tony closed his mouth and turned, wide eyed, to Anna and Dario.

Anna threw her arms around him. "I can't believe it."

With his free arm, Tony grabbed his uncle and embraced him.

Durante wrapped his arms around Anna and Tony. He stepped back and pointed to a weathered house standing among trees. "See the house, over there?"

"Yes, near the olive trees."

Durante nodded. "That was your father's house."

Anna pressed herself against Tony and squeezed his hand.

"Your father sent you?" Durante asked.

"Yes, he's worried."

Durante's jaw tightened. "Is he in good health?"

"Yes."

Durante motioned to Anna and Dario. "And these are your friends?"

"I'm sorry. This is Anna and her cousin Dario. They saved my life."

Durante kissed Anna's cheeks and hugged Dario. "Do you live near here?"

"Yes, in the valley, near Pezzano," Anna said.

Durante tilted his head and spent the next few seconds staring at the stone wall. He glanced at Anna. "What is your family name?"

"Amati," she said.

Durante straightened, adding two inches to his height. "Amati... olive oil. Do you know a man named Luca Amati?"

Anna's hand covered her mouth. "He's my uncle!"

A wide grin came over Durante's face. "My wife's brother sells olives to him."

Anna froze, then grabbed Tony's shirt and pulled him to her side.

"Are you happy?" Tony asked.

Anna looked up at him and smiled. "Today it's the best day of my life."

"Is there a place I can buy food?" Tony asked, his uncle.

"Yes, a small market near here."

Tony turned to Dario and grinned. "You think Luca will start the family olive oil business again?"

"Yes, soon."

"You met one of your suppliers."

The two men smiled at each other.

Tony placed an arm around Anna and pulled her against his side. He pointed at his father's house. "When the war ends, our children will be born in that house?"

Anna grabbed his collar, pulled him down and kissed him. "I can't wait."

Durante, Tony, Anna, and Dario walked to the jeep.

Dario put an arm over Tony's shoulder. Anna held on to Durante's arm and leaned against him.

Tony patted Dario on his cheek and smiled.

THE END

In September 1943, Amadeo Castagno, a paratrooper in Bravo Company, 1st Battalion, 504th Parachute Infantry Regiment jumped into Italy, outside the city of Salerno. He hoped to contact his father's family in the mountains southeast of the city. The battles fought between Salerno and Anzio kept him away from the small town of Filetta di San Cipriano Picentini.

It wasn't until March 21, 1944, that he left Naples and travel south toward Salerno. The evening before his departure, lava and ash from the eruption of Mount Vesuvius forced the closure of the road between the two cities, making the trip impossible. Chief Warrant Officer Amadeo Castagno made that journey, and met his Uncle Durante, beside a fountain in the small town of Filetta, in the summer of 1959.

www.ingramcontent.com/pod-product-compliance
Lightning Source LLC
Chambersburg PA
CBHW071252130626
46556CB00003B/1279